TEACHING HIS BABYGIRL

The Playground Series

RORY REYNOLDS

Copyright © 2021 by Rory Reynolds

All rights reserved.

No part of this book may be reproduced in any form or by any electronic or mechanical means, including information storage and retrieval systems, without written permission from the author, except for the use of brief quotations in a book review.

Cover by PopKitty Designs

❦ Created with Vellum

Move to a new city. Check.
New amazing job. Check.
Land belly down over a stranger's knee... a super hot, really dominant stranger?

Double check.

He's strong and stubborn, stern and unyielding... Colton James is the kind of daddy that's dangerous to my heart.

After just one taste of his firm hand, just one night... I want more. I should turn back, but now it's too late. I'm in too deep.

Only problem? He's my new boss and is completely off-limits.

Sign up for Rory Reynolds newsletter and never miss a release. Sign up here or go to www.roryreynoldsromance.com

PROLOGUE

"I don't like it," Charity says for the fifth time.

I blow out a breath of frustration. I love that she's concerned for me, but at the same time, I'm not the fresh-faced submissive she met all those years ago. I'm twenty-seven, almost twenty-eight; this isn't my first rodeo.

"Charity, I appreciate the concern, I really do, but I'll be fine. It's not like I'm meeting some dom on a dating app and heading to his house. This is a club. A club with excellent security, I might add."

I can practically hear Charity's mind whirring as she tries to come up with yet another excuse why going to a club alone is such a bad idea. "Why did you have to move so far away?" she finally asks.

My lips turn up into a sad smile. "You know Thurston Academy was too good an opportunity to pass up. They have a top-notch art department, and I'll be the head of the program.

"You were the head of Colson's art program too," she huffs.

I can't hold my laughter at bay. "Yeah, the art program of one—me. Not to mention the tiny art room and zero funding. You know this is the opportunity of a lifetime. We already discussed it... Hell, you *encouraged* me to move."

She lets out a loud sigh. I can imagine her throwing herself back on her couch dramatically. "I guess when I was busy encouraging you to chase your dreams, I didn't realize I would be losing my best friend."

"You haven't lost me. You're stuck with me for life. Like a barnacle that has to be scraped from the sides of ships. I'm going nowhere."

"Psh, just halfway across the country."

My smile fades, and a wave of homesickness overcomes me. "I miss you too, Cha-cha. I've got to finish getting ready..."

"Okay, fine. Just promise me you'll be careful. No creepers."

"I think that's something I can easily promise."

"Good. I love you, Dar. I hope you know that I'm proud of you, even if I whine about missing you and hating that you're gone."

I smile at that. "I know. I love you too. I'll call you tomorrow and give you the deets of my first trip to The Playground."

"You better!"

We say our goodbyes, and then I finish getting ready—time to start phase two of my brand-new life.

Phase one: Dream job.

Phase two: Dream dominant. A daddy, specifically.
Phase three: Happily ever after.
Easy peasy...

CHAPTER ONE

Darlene

THE PLAYGROUND ISN'T AS busy as I thought it would be, but it's early yet. I came early so that I could look around a bit before my appointment with the guide assigned to me. Once I start taking in the main areas of the club, I'm glad I came in early. It's a lot to take in.

I can't help but smile at the stark differences between this club and other BDSM clubs I've visited over the years. Most are dark and have an edge to them... the central area of this club is brightly lit and decorated in purples and blues with black and silver highlights. It's basically the opposite of the standard black leather most clubs gravitate towards.

There are other—bigger—differences. For example, the large playground in the middle of the room that gives the club its name, complete with a swing set and sandbox. There are two littles playing on the jungle gym while their daddy and mommy doms watch on with indulgent smiles on their faces. I watch for a while, then move on to see the area I will think of as the punishment area.

This part is more like a standard BDSM club, though, admittedly more colorful. The leather of the spanking benches is in varying shades of white, blue, and pink. The cuffs for the St. Andrew's crosses are also colorful. In fact, all of the pieces of equipment have some extra flair to them. The most significant difference is the many triangular shaped spaces that are clearly recreations of corners. A punishment that is on my least favorite list—corner time. I would much rather take a good belting to sitting in a corner, staring at the wall. Boring.

I wander around, taking in the more private areas. Some are occupied with couples acting out their fantasies. I linger at one where a woman is thrown over a large man's lap as he paddles her. I can't hear what he's telling her, but I can imagine he's scolding her for whatever infraction she committed. My heart clenches in my chest at that. I want someone who will hold me accountable. Someone who will care enough to set rules and enforce them.

My sigh is a sad one. Is it too much to ask for a dominant to love me? Someone that I can trust to never hurt me and to only want what's best for me. Someone loyal, not like the jerks I've dated in the past. I'm starting to wonder if it's me that's the problem. I'm not especially bratty, but I do have a strong will, and it takes a strong dominant to go up against it. I know it does, but surely there's a man out there that's up to the task.

I ignore the private rooms; part of my tour includes a

closer look at them, and for now, I just want to get a feel for the place before my official tour starts.

The opposite side of the club has an area dedicated to different stations for littles to play together at. Dollhouses, trains and cars, a bookshelf full of board games and puzzles, an area that looks like it's entirely dedicated to art projects... the only thing I would ever be interested in when it comes to this stuff.

Don't get me wrong... I have a favorite stuffie and love dressing up like a girly-girl, but dollhouses just aren't me. I'm not into age-play. I can understand why some people are. I can imagine how freeing it could be to regress into a simpler time, but it's not my thing.

After taking everything in, I end up back where I started—a plush area filled with overstuffed couches and dozens of pillows. The person who let me in explained the different areas of the club briefly... this is a waiting room of sorts. Littles and dominants can hang out in this area to let it be known that they are looking for a play partner for the night. There are several men and women chatting amicably. They all look like they know each other—and they probably do. Clubs like this tend to be fairly exclusive in their members. I can imagine in a place like this, the people would start to feel like family after a while.

I consider the couches for a moment longer before heading to the bar where I'm supposed to meet my guide. The bar is perfectly balanced to serve both littles and their dominants. There are juices and slushy machines beside high-end liquor. Colorful plastic cups alongside crystal cut tumblers and wine glasses. It's a perfect representation of the juxtaposition between daddy and little.

The bar area is empty, save for the woman behind the bar and a man nursing a drink at the opposite end of the bar as me. I walk up to the bar and take a seat on one of the empty stools.

"What can I get you, princess?" the bartender asks.

"Can I just have water, please?"

She looks at me like I'm insane but grabs a bottle from behind the bar and opens it for me.

"Thanks."

"You're welcome. I'm Tessa," she says, assessing me.

"Darlene," I say with a small smile.

"Nice to meet ya. Is this your first time at the club?"

"Yeah. Is it that obvious?"

She shrugs. "You just have that touristy feel to ya."

Not sure what to say to that, I take a drink.

"Tessa, leave the girl alone," the man from the end of the bar barks, looking dark and imposing.

Tessa's friendly demeanor changes in the blink of an eye. Her eyes are green fire when she turns to level a glare at the man. "Shut up, Ransom. No one asked you," she hisses.

He gives her a meaningful look—the kind that promises a sore ass and a very unhappy little girl at the end of the night—and she stomps her foot, crossing her arms over her chest. "I'm allowed to talk to people. It's kind of my job."

"Talk, yes. Torment, no."

Tessa looks at me and must see something that I don't because her temper disappears as quickly as it came. "Sorry... I just meant that I haven't seen you around before," she says to me, looking every bit the chastised little girl.

"It's okay," I reply, but Tessa isn't paying any attention to me; she's looking over my shoulder with an almost dreamy look on her face. I turn to see what she's looking at and am completely blindsided by the most attractive man I've ever seen in my life.

Blond hair, icy blue eyes... a strong chiseled jaw covered in a two-day scruff. He's a little over six foot, and I can tell that he's got the body of a god under his expensive suit. The man is sex on a stick, as Charity would say. And he's heading straight for me. I sit up straighter on the stool and adjust the skirt of my dress.

Tessa gives the man a huge, welcoming smile. "Colt! It's so good to see you. It's been forever. What are you doing here?"

"Good evening, Tessa. I'm here for a favor to Aiden. He had a thing tonight and needed someone to cover his tour."

Goosebumps shiver down my spine at the low rumble of his voice. My nipples peak, and my thighs clench together. Since when has just the sound of a man's voice turned me on so much? It takes a few seconds to realize what he said... is this my guide? If so, lucky me.

Very lucky me...

Holy crap, he even smells fantastic like expensive scotch—woodsy with a hit of something else I can't quite name. Basically, the man is a wet dream in the flesh. My long-dormant little side comes raring to the surface, ready to play.

"Colt, meet Darlene," Tessa says, introducing us.

Colt turns his attention to me for the first time, leveling those icy eyes on me. I shift in my seat, nervous under all of his attention. I mentally shake myself. This isn't me. I'm not some wilting flower that goes all gaga for a man she doesn't know. I roll back my shoulders and take a deep breath, finding my hard-won confidence.

I bravely stick my hand out for him to shake. "Nice to meet-" My words cut off when instead of shaking my hand, he brings it up to his lips and brushes his lips over my knuckles. His short beard tickles my skin, the firm softness of his lips on me sends a tremor through me.

"The pleasure is all mine, I assure you," Colt says, turning my hand and pressing a kiss to the inside of my wrist before releasing me.

My entire body jerks to attention, my core clenching and my nipples tightening. One tiny touch from this man has me a needy mess. Desperate for more touches. More kisses. I imagine that wicked mouth of his elsewhere. I shake myself out of my fantasies. That's not what tonight is about. Tonight is about touring the club and its inner workings to decide if this is the place for me. From what I've seen so far, I'm convinced I could definitely have fun here. It's way more appealing than any of the standard clubs I've ever been to.

"Are you ready for your tour?" Colt says in that sexy rumble of his.

Goodbye panties.

I paste on my brightest smile, trying to hide just how much he's affecting me.

"Yes, sir," I say in deference to his dominant status, remembering my manners despite the fact that my brain is currently on hiatus.

His lips tip up in a grin that gives me yet another thing to find sexy about him. Colt holds out his hand, and I put mine in his so he can help me down from the stool… he doesn't release me right away. In fact, he doesn't truly release me at all because he moves my hand to the crook of his elbow and guides me away from the bar.

I turn and look at Tessa, who is staring at our retreat with shocked eyes. It makes me wonder if this is abnormal behavior for Colt… and why does that send a little thrill through me?

CHAPTER TWO

Colt

SHOWING a new prospective member around the club isn't exactly what I wanted to do with my Friday night, but it's better than another lonely night at home. Besides, it's been months since I've been to The Playground. Maybe after the tour I can find a nice little girl to take over my knee for the night. Even thinking it doesn't bring me any kind of anticipation. Playing with one of the single submissives used to be enough to scratch the itch, but now all it does is make me long for more.

I never thought I would be tempted to settle down, especially after my breakup with Trisha, but lately, I find myself craving something more permanent. A temporary arrangement just doesn't appeal like it once did.

The club is still quiet compared to how it will be later tonight. Apparently, my charge is shy and doesn't want to tour while things are in full swing. Unusual. Most people want to see the club at capacity. I mentally shrug. It's early enough that I will have plenty of time after the tour to get myself in the mood to find someone to have a scene with—scratch the itch that's been untouchable so far.

Even the bar area where people gather to talk and catch up is empty. Tessa is behind the bar, and one of the security monitors—Ransom—is sitting at one end of the bar. At the other end is a fucking angel. I hasten my steps, wanting to get a better look at the woman. I've never seen her at the club before... is this my charge? All of a sudden, my night is looking that much brighter.

Tessa shouts a greeting, and the angel turns to watch my approach. She's even more beautiful than I thought now that I fully see her. The woman has my cock rock-hard in my slacks, and I'm ready to fall to my knees and worship the sweet heaven between her thighs.

Big brown eyes take me in almost warily, but she can't hide the spark of attraction. Is it possible she feels the same draw I do? Could a man be so lucky? I slow my steps, taking in more of my—because she will be mine—beauty. She's got long brown hair that has waves that look untamable. She's got a pert little nose and full, cupids bow lips. Lips that it takes all of my self-control not to take in a kiss the second I'm within touching distance.

Her sweet citrus scent floods my senses, and I'm barely aware that Tessa is talking. I respond by rote, unable to take my eyes off the beauty in front of me.

"Colt, meet Darlene," Tessa says with a hint of amusement at my obvious infatuation with the woman.

Darlene holds her hand out for me to shake. I take her small hand in mine and lean over it, lightly kissing her knuckles, cutting off her 'nice to meet you.' She stutters and can't seem to find the words. Her breath hitches when I turn her hand and press a seductive kiss to the inside of her wrist, tasting her sweetness.

She shivers at my touch, obviously as taken with me as I am her. I thank my lucky stars because if she's as physically aware of me as I am her, maybe this evening won't end nearly as poorly as I expected. Darlene's the first woman I've felt such an attraction to in longer than I can remember—maybe ever.

"Are you ready for your tour?" I'm not sure how I know she's the one I'm supposed to show around, but I just do. If I believed in fate, I would think that's what's brought us together tonight.

"Yes, sir," she says respectfully. What I wouldn't give for her to call me daddy instead.

I take her hand in mine and help her from the stool. When she moves to pull away, I don't release her. I place her soft hand on the crook of my elbow and lead her out into the club proper. She looks up at me with a small smile. I tell myself that she'd give the same smile to anyone who showed her the proper respect of a gentleman, but part of me thinks that soft smile is just for me.

Silence stretches between us as I slowly walk her around the club. I realize too late that I should be explaining the different areas and letting her ask questions. She seems content to just walk around with me taking things in. I finally shake myself out of my lust-filled stupor and start doing my job.

"This area is what we call the toybox." I indicate the area directly in front of us with different stations for the littles to play together or with their daddies and mommies. "Would you like to stop and play?"

Her nose scrunches up. "Playing with toys doesn't appeal to me," she says bluntly.

"Not all littles enjoy it," I say, patting her hand encouragingly. Liking that she already knows exactly who she is as a submissive. She might be new to this club, but she's obviously not a new submissive.

I walk her over to the large playground where the club gets its name. "This one is pretty obvious…"

She giggles, the sound like tinkling bells. My cock throbs again at the sound. Fuck, everything about this woman is perfect. "I do like to swing," she says shyly. "But it's been years."

"Do you want to?" I ask, giving her an encouraging look. I want to give this woman anything she wants. If she wants to spend the rest of the night swinging, I will gladly stand by and watch her enjoy herself.

She gives a quick shake of her head. "No, thank you. I would rather continue the tour… if you don't mind?"

"Not at all, beauty." I give her hand another pat and lead her on to the next area. "This area is obviously where punishments happen," I say, indicating the spanking benches and other equipment.

Darlene purses her lips… "And funishments?" she asks.

I smirk down at her. "And funishments," I agree.

She smiles playfully. "I like those more than swinging."

Is she hinting that she wants me to spank her? I have to force myself to pull her away from temptation. This is her first time at the club; she deserves better than her guide to jump on her like a rabid animal.

"Over here is the restaurant. While you can bring

non-club members to eat, they aren't allowed beyond this door. There's another entrance on the opposite side for people to enter from the street."

She gives me a nod, but doesn't show much interest, her attention seems to be drawn toward the area where the private rooms are at. I inwardly smirk.

"This hall leads to the private rooms."

She gives me a heated look, one that spells trouble for my self-control. I should skip this part of the tour, but I can't seem to make myself listen to reason. I start at the far end of the hallway then start walking her through the rooms. The first two are more masculine in nature. Decorated to look and feel like a daddy's bedroom. The next is full of trains and other toys that would appeal to a little boy. The next two are directed more toward punishments and look slightly more like the private rooms of standard BDSM clubs. She doesn't show any interest in any of them.

Then we get to the last room, and her excitement sparks. She twirls around the white and pink room like it's a wonderland. And it is. This room is girly and decorated with silhouettes from Alice in Wonderland characters. The colors and décor are all in the same theme.

Darlene turns to me with a huge smile. "I love Alice!"

I meet her smile with one of my own. "I'm glad. I was starting to think you didn't find anything about the private rooms enjoyable."

"I liked them okay, but this one is the best."

I chuckle at her excitement. It's the most animated she's been throughout the entire tour. Her happiness is contagious, and I find myself feeling lighter than I have in years. "This is the last part of our tour," I say, hating that I'm putting an end to our time together. "Is there anything else you'd like to see? I could maybe... introduce you to some people." The words feel like barbed wire in my throat. I absolutely don't want to introduce her to anyone. I want to keep her to myself.

"I—um—well..." she stutters.

"You can ask for anything," I say, closing the small distance between us, stopping just in front of her. And I do mean anything. I'm pretty sure I could deny her nothing.

"What if what I want is you?" she asks boldly, even as she shyly looks down at her feet.

I definitely didn't plan this. I hoped for it but never thought she would be so bold, despite her obvious confidence, to ask for a scene. She doesn't seem the type to ask a virtual stranger for a scene, let alone a stranger in a private room.

It takes my brain a moment to catch up with exactly what's happening here. I know one thing; I can't turn her away. Not now, not ever.

Darlene stands demurely in the middle of the room. Her fingers threaded together in front of her as she looks down at her shoes. She's a vision as she awaits my response. I close the rest of the distance between us, and with a finger under her chin, I lift her eyes to mine.

"When we talked, you told me that you weren't looking to jump into scenes with random daddies."

She chews her lip, thinking about her response. "You don't feel like just some random daddy dom to me. Is that crazy?"

I shake my head. "No, I understand exactly what you mean." I look at her meaningfully, bringing my lips to hers. Our kiss is slow and exploring. She presses her lush curves to mine, her soft tongue lightly licking at my lips, asking to deepen the kiss. I open to her, letting her seeking tongue explore for a moment before I take control.

With my fingers laced through her hair, I tilt her head back, deepening the kiss. Where her tongue was soft and exploring, mine is bold and possessive. I kiss her like I own her. Like she's mine and mine alone. This might be just one night, just one scene, but I'll be damned if I hold back any of this pent-up desire from her.

Darlene grips the lapels of my jacket, pressing her sweet curves even closer to me. My cock is so hard it aches with wanting inside her slick heat. I wrestle back control over myself. She asked for a scene, not for me to fall on her like a savage beast. I refuse to take advantage of her desires. After watching others' play in the club and the constant flirting between us, she's not clearheaded. I won't leave her needy and wanting, but I also won't seek out my own pleasure.

Not tonight. Soon though. This night is all for her.

I shrug off my suit jacket, never letting our lips part. I guide her back towards the bed. I finally break our kiss when her knees bump the edge of the bed. Her lids are heavy, and her breaths are coming in short pants. I slowly lower the zipper at the back of her dress and let it fall to the floor, so it pools around her ankles. She stands before me in nothing but white lace.

"Fuck, you're a vision, Darlene."

She chews her bottom lip, flushing a fetching shade of pink at my compliment. It tells me she doesn't hear it enough. I run my knuckles between her full breasts and down over her soft stomach, showing her how much I love her curvy body without words. I grip her rounded hips and pull her against me so she feels my hardness. My lips steal another kiss; my hunger for her won't be denied.

"Tell me what you want, sweet girl," I growl against her lips.

She looks at me with hungry eyes. "I want to be spanked..."

I let out another low growl. "By who?"

"You... daddy," she says, pausing briefly before she uses the title that makes my cock ache. I want to be her daddy, and not just for the moment.

I take a step back and slowly start to roll up my shirt sleeves, watching Darlene's eyes dilate. Anticipation rolls through me. Her lovely breasts rise and fall as her breaths become heavy, her own anticipation growing. She watches as I take a seat on the end of the bed and pat my lap. Without hesitating, she lays herself over my knee, ready for her spanking. I run my palm over the silky soft skin of her back, then down over her lace-covered ass and back again. Over and over, I pet her body until she's relaxed and pliant under my ministrations.

"Such a beautiful canvas to paint red with my handprint."

She lets out a low moan, followed by a whimper as I tug her panties down below her ass. I groan at the wet way they stick to her pussy. My cock jumps in my slacks, begging for attention. She feels my hardness and squirms against my length, causing precome to drip from my cock. The first spank is part warning, part punishment for driving me crazy. She stills instantly.

"Behave, little girl."

"S-sorry, daddy. You're just so..." she trails off as if she can't find the right adjective to describe what she feels.

"I'm just so fucking hard and achy for your hot cunt. That's what I am."

"Yes... that..." she breathes the words. Her hips wriggle impatiently, begging me for more spanks.

I spank her again, and she moans. I keep spanking her until I hear her sniffle. I stop and rub out the pain until she's writhing on my lap, her pussy soaked and needy. Unable to help myself, I gently run my fingers through all that wetness. She's drenched. She pushes back into my fingers, desperate for my touch. I circle her clit, giving her what she wants.

"Please, oh God, daddy!"

I enter her tight sheath with two fingers, wishing it was my cock. I keep rubbing her clit with my thumb as she moves against my hand, trying to steal her release from me. I slap her thighs in warning, and she stills.

"Good girl," I praise. "You're so fucking wet... did my girl's naughty little pussy like her punishment?"

"No, daddy," Darlene whimpers. We both know that's a lie. She loved her spanking. "It hurt."

"I bet," I say, rubbing the abused flesh of her ass. "Your ass is a beautiful shade of red. Marked by *my* hand."

I lay another three spanks on her upturned ass. She both whimpers and moans as the pain and pleasure meld together.

"You love it, though. Don't you, babygirl?"

"Yes, daddy. I love it when you spank me," she admits.

My cock leaks even more at the sincerity in her voice—I can almost believe that I'm her daddy and not just a temporary partner—what will it take to convince this beautiful woman to give me a real chance? Whatever it takes, I'm going to do it. I'm going to claim her as my own. It'll be my handprints on her ass. My hands that hold her heart. I can't explain this instant connection between us, but I'm not going to question it, and I won't turn my back on it.

Darlene is mine.

I deliver two more spanks, then move back to rubbing her clit. She arches her back, pushing against my hand. "Please..." she pleads.

This time I don't stop. I thrust two fingers inside her, hitting her g-spot as I rub her clit. I fuck her with my hand until she's crying out her orgasm. Even then, I don't stop. I keep rubbing and fucking her with my fingers until she's screaming for mercy; only then do I relent. She lays over my lap completely limp—sated. My cock aches. I remind myself that this is only for her and that there will be a next time where I'll fuck her sweet pussy until we're both sated.

I lift her off my lap and arrange her on the big bed. She shivers in the slight chill of the room. I crawl into bed behind her, pulling her into my arms. I feel like I could take on the whole world when she snuggles into me.

"You okay?" I quietly ask.

"Mmm... so good," she murmurs. "Thank you, Colt."

I want to correct her. I want to hear her call me

daddy again. But I bite my tongue. I'm not her daddy yet, and our scene is done. I press a kiss to the top of her head. "You're welcome, babygirl. It was my pleasure."

She wriggles her bottom against my hard length. I pinch her nipple through the lace of her bra. "Naughty girl, stop teasing."

"It doesn't have to be a tease…"

I cup her cheek and turn her face to mine. "I love that you want to do that for me, but tonight was all about you."

"But–"

"No buts. I won't take advantage of you. If you still want me next time… then there will be no stopping me from claiming your tight cunt. It'll be mine."

She blinks up at me with lustful eyes. "Next time…"

"Yes, next time," I growl. "Next weekend. If you want more, meet me here Saturday night."

Darlene closes her eyes with a small smile and snuggles into my hold. Even though I'm still desperately hard, it's made more bearable by the knowledge that she's just as excited for next time as I am.

CHAPTER THREE
Darlene

THE WEEKEND FLIES by in a flurry of unpacking boxes and daydreaming about Colt. I've never in my life felt so instantly connected to another person. It's scary how in sync we were Friday night. Needless to say, we made plans for this coming weekend. I think I'm more excited about that than I am about starting my new job. Which I'm going to be late for if I don't get in gear and leave.

The school is only a five-block walk from my apartment. Even though there is a chill in the air, I decide to walk. A little exercise might work off some of the sexual tension that's kept me on a hair-trigger since Friday night when Colt walked me to my car and kissed me half to death.

Just thinking about it has me feeling hot under the collar. I take off my heels and drop them in my bag and slip on my flats for the walk. I take a big breath of the crisp fall air and sigh. I love fall. The wind is colder than I thought, and I regret not bringing my coat as a chill runs through me. I consider turning around for my car but don't. The school is just ahead, looming tall over the surrounding buildings.

I take in the school, pausing briefly to enjoy the beauty of it. Thurston Academy is a three-story brick masterpiece. It looks almost like a castle with an old-world charm. It gives the same feel as any of the many Ivy League schools that populate the east coast.

I nearly lose my footing when someone bumps into my back. A student with a letterman's jacket mumbles an apology as he lumbers into the building. I spent so long admiring my new place of employment that I didn't realize that the school was starting to fill up with students. I shake my head at my silliness and head into the building.

Excitement courses through me as I pull open the doors and head to the office to collect my class rosters.

"Miss Larson!" Judy, the administrative assistant, says happily. "So good to see you again."

"Darlene, please," I correct with a smile. "How was your weekend, Judy?"

"Darlene, then," she says with a smile. "It was good. Just puttered around in the garden with my husband John. What about you? Did you get unpacked?"

My cheeks heat with a blush at the reminder of just how little I got done this weekend. I couldn't concentrate on anything and spent half the weekend daydreaming with my fingers in my panties. "Eh, some... You know how it is."

She laughs. "That I do. I hate unpacking. It's the worst part of moving."

I nod in agreement.

"Oh," she snaps her fingers. "You're here for your

class rosters, and I'm just over here jabbering your ear off when you need to get ready before first period."

She quickly goes through the folders on her desk, finding the one that's marked with my name and handing it to me.

"You know where you're going, right?"

"Yep." I look towards the principal's darkened office, thinking it's weird that he hasn't introduced himself yet. I was here twice last week, and he wasn't here either time. Maybe things are just done differently in the city. The principal of my own school handled new hires and school tours on his own. Thurston Academy has a huge school board that seems to make all the hiring decisions.

"Is Mr. James in?" I ask curiously.

"He's around here somewhere. He likes to walk the halls in the mornings. Have you met him yet?"

I shake my head. "No, he wasn't here when I came in Friday to prep my room."

"Well, you'll meet him today, I'm sure."

A harried-looking teacher rushes into the room, and Judy turns her attention to her. "Melinda, whatever is the matter?"

"I locked myself out of my room. I need the master key," she pants.

I wave at Judy and take my leave so I can get my bearings before class starts.

THE FIRST TWO classes go without a hitch... the third not so much. "Mr. Zimmerman, would you like to tell the whole class what you're whispering about?" I ask after the fourth time he's interrupted my lecture.

His friend slaps his shoulder and eggs him on, encouraging him to tell the class whatever he was saying. I suddenly regret the threat, especially when he turns to look at me, and I recognize the heated look in his eyes.

"I was just wondering if your pussy tastes like cherry pie, Miss Larson."

My jaw drops as the rest of the class is half gasps and half riotous laughter. In all my years of teaching, I have never had anyone say something so inappropriate to me. I'm stunned into silence.

"Well, does it?" One of the other boys asks.

That shakes me out of my stupor. "Mr. Zimmerman and Mr. Yardley, principal's office now." They both high-five on their way out the door. The rest of the class sits in stunned silence as if they can't believe what just happened. I know I sure can't.

I mean, what the actual fuck. Since when do students talk to teachers like that? Thankfully the bell rings, and I can dismiss my class. I take a couple steadying breaths before making my way down to the office. I don't want those idiot boys trying to downplay what happened.

Judy gives me a puzzled look when she sees me. Her eyes flashing between the two boys sitting in front of the closed door to Mr. James' office and me. "Hello, Judy. Is Mr. James free? Mr. Zimmerman and Mr. Yardly and I need to have a little chat about classroom decorum."

"He's ready for you."

I give her a bright smile. "Thank you, Judy." I turn to the boys and wave my hand between them and the door. "Gentlemen, if you would."

"Todd, Leon... What brings you to my office on the first day of school?" A familiar voice asks from inside the office. My heart starts to race as I close the door and step around the boys. I gasp in shock as I take in Colt sitting behind a big wooden desk, looking every part the stern disciplinarian.

"Darlene," Colt says, equally as shocked at my appearance as I am at having just walked into his office. He clears his throat. "Miss Larson," he quickly corrects himself.

"Mr. James," I say with a nod of deference to his position. "It seems that Mr. Zimmerman and Mr. Yardley need a lesson in respect."

He raises his brow at the acid in my tone. Both boys have their shoulders hunched and are looking very much like petulant children.

"Is that true, boys?"

They both shrug their shoulders.

"Why don't you tell Mr. James exactly what you said, Mr. Zimmerman," I say with a benevolent smile. A smile that says I'm very much going to enjoy what's about to happen.

Neither of the boys makes a move to say anything, which is unsurprising. I wouldn't want to be called out in front of Colt James either. He's looking especially stern —and sexy—today. Unfortunately, my pussy agrees, and I'm finding myself horny on top of being angry about the disrespectful kids we're here for.

I clear my throat, trying to shake off the memories from Friday night. "Well, boys, will you tell him, or should I?" I ask, feeling vindicated at their obvious embarrassment in the face of a man like Colt. He's the kind of man that demands respect, and I can only imagine his reaction.

"Alright, then. Let's see if I can recall correctly," I say to Mr. Zimmerman. The boy cringes back like I just verbally smacked him. He doesn't think I'll say it... I know what he's thinking. The buttoned-up art teacher will shy away, and they'll be off the hook. He'd be wrong. I may dress the part of a conservative woman to the outside world, but inside I'm wild and untamed. "You'll correct me if I'm wrong, won't you?" I ask innocently, making both boys cringe again.

This is too much fun, really. I've moved on from anger to enjoying watching them squirm like fish on a hook.

"Mr. Zimmerman here was wondering if my pussy tastes like cherry pie, and Mr. Yardley seconded his musings."

Colt's icy blue eyes turn furious as he slams his hands on his desk, rising from his seat like an avenging angel.

"You what?!" he bellows, looking between the boys and me. A possessive fury is written on his features as plain as day. I hope the boys only see it as outrage and not the protectiveness it appears to be.

Maybe I'm just seeing things that aren't there. Wishful thinking is what it is... what it has to be. Which is stupid now that it's finally sinking in that Colt is, for all intents and purposes, my new boss and entirely off-limits. No matter how much I want him, it just can't happen. I can't risk messing up my new job. Even if it means giving up something that I spent every minute of every day obsessing over since he kissed me goodbye Friday night.

"I cannot believe you would say something like that," Colt says, reining in his anger slightly. "The disrespect you've shown Miss Larson, on her first day no less, is utterly appalling."

"Sorry, Mr. James," both boys parrot.

"It's not me you should be apologizing to." He points my direction, and both boys turn to me with repentant expressions. Obviously, these boys respect Colt and hate that they've disappointed him.

"Sorry, Miss Larson," they both say together, making it almost comical.

"I would say it's okay, but it isn't. I can forgive this little misunderstanding, though, provided you never speak to a woman that way again."

"We won't. We promise."

I don't believe them for a second, but I can hope they understand words have consequences and what they said is absolutely wrong.

"Now that Miss Larson has magnanimously forgiven you, your punishment is that you'll be sitting out the next two games."

Both boys groan and open their mouths to protest, but they both fall silent with a raise of Colt's hand. "And you get to explain to coach exactly why you have to sit out."

"He's going to kill us," Leon says.

"It would be well deserved after your behavior today, but we all know you're only going to be running drills... lots of drills," Colt says with a malevolent smile.

I smirk at the look Colt gives me and know that they're going to be well punished, more punished than any suspension from school would provide. Hopefully, it will be enough to really hit home the consequences for their actions, but only time will tell.

"You boys get on to class. Miss Larson, if I could have a word..."

My eyes widen at the firmness in his tone. He probably sensed my desire to bolt as soon as this conversation ended. He wouldn't be wrong. The sooner we talk, the sooner I have to admit that things can't proceed with our budding relationship. I know it was only one night—one scene—but it felt like so much more. I've never felt such a connection with another person in all of my life.

I don't want it to end, but what choice do I have?

CHAPTER FOUR

Colt

WHEN SHE FIRST ENTERED THE office, I was shocked to find out that the new art teacher is my Darlene. The woman I've spent the whole weekend lusting after. Leon and Todd are lucky to be leaving this office without being pummeled. No one talks to my girl like that. The only one who should think about what her sweet pussy tastes like is me.

As soon as the boys leave, I'm striding around the desk and locking the door to my office. She's watching me warily like I'm some kind of feral animal that's about to pounce. She wouldn't be wrong. I am about to pounce. I've been without her lips for two days too long. Darlene takes a step back, and I growl low in my throat, not liking her backing away from me. Before she can take another step, I've got her wrapped up in my arms, her curvy body pressed against the hard plains of mine.

She stands stiff in my arms until I wrap her hair around my fist and tip her head back. Her eyes fall closed, and her lips part as she awaits my kiss. I bypass her lips, going instead to her neck. I lick and suck the delicate skin, enjoying the salty-sweet flavor of her. Darlene lets out a low moan that I steal away with a fierce kiss.

For the briefest of moments, she's stiff in my arms, but then she melts. Her soft tongue licks at mine as I plunder her mouth. Ravaging any bit of hesitance she has away. With hands fisted in my shirt, she holds me to her, kissing me back like she's starved for it. Our tongues dance together, mine possessive and hers sweet and seeking. She lets me lead with low whimpers and moans.

My hands roam over her body, lifting her skirt up so that I can grip the round globes of her ass through the simple cotton panties she's wearing. I itch to spank her but don't dare because if I do, I won't stop until my cock is buried deep inside her wet heat.

Darlene rips her lips from mine, pushing me away. She couldn't actually move me if she tried, but I take a step back, not wanting to make her feel caged entirely—even if she is. Her breasts rise and fall as she desperately sucks in air like she's seconds away from drowning. I move to grab her up again, but she raises her hands and takes a step back to ward me off.

"We can't..." she says, her fingers coming to her lips as if to silence her own protests. It's like she knows if she doesn't keep them there, she will lose control and fall into me all over again despite her own resolve to deny us this reunion.

"We can, babygirl," I growl possessively.

"You're my boss!" she whisper-shouts. "Don't you know what that means?"

"What does it mean?" I ask, stalking her as she backs away.

"This can't happen," she waves her hands between us, "us—whatever this connection is—it can't... we can't."

"We can... we will," I practically snarl the words as I back her against the wall. "There's no rule that says we can't."

I brush my lips lightly over hers, and she whimpers. Her head thumping against the wall as she tries to pull away. I chase her lips with my own until it's her that's kissing me. We catch fire. Burning bright as our tongues seek out one another and the kiss ignites all of the pent-up passion from Friday night.

We break apart again, her eyes heavy-lidded. She licks her lips, savoring the taste of our kiss. "People won't respect me," she whispers. "They'll think..."

Darlene shakes her head, ducks under my arm, and flees my office.

Runaway, little girl... daddy isn't afraid of a little chase.

CHAPTER FIVE
Darlene

THE WEEK FLIES BY. I've somehow managed to avoid being alone with Colt, despite his many attempts to corner me. It's only a matter of time before it happens though. Each time I see him, it becomes harder to resist him. Not that I even want to resist him... I want him more than I've ever wanted anyone in my life.

I take another glass from the box sitting on my kitchen floor and give it a quick rinse before filling it with orange juice. I consider adding some vodka but don't. Alcohol will only make the situation that much worse. I lean against the counter as I sip my juice. The place is still full of boxes. The only room I've unpacked is my studio... which I've spent every night after school painting.

I finish my juice and wander back into my studio. Icy blue eyes meet me. Despite trying to paint something else... each painting this week ends up with icy blue eyes and the stern features of Colt James. They burn through me from the canvas.

My eyes flick to the clock and my insides twist. I'm supposed to meet Colt at the club in an hour. But that was before... I've vacillated between my decision to go or not go for days now. Finally, making the wise choice to not go. Now that the time is upon me, I'm second-guessing my decision.

One more night couldn't hurt... In fact, we could work this thing out of our systems... that's what we need to do. We will sate this undeniable need, and it'll be over.

Right?

Even though it's probably the worst decision, I change my mind. I'm going. Come what may.

I take a quick shower, washing off the paint, and shaving every inch of my body. I pull on my favorite pink satin and lace bra with matching boy short panties. I turn and look in the mirror admiring my curves. I might not be a skinny girl, but even I can admit my curves are sexy. I have an hourglass figure—large breasts with a nipped-in waist and curvy hips.

With a hum, I pull on a frilly pink dress over my lingerie and slide my feet into my favorite ballerina slippers. I may choose heels and conservative dresses in my day-to-day life, but I shed that protective outer layer for the club. I no longer look like that put together teacher, I look like the little I am. In these clothes, I feel like me.

I let go of the confines of society and can just be unapologetically me. I let out a sigh, feeling free for the first time in what feels like forever.

The club is packed. Obviously, Saturday night starts earlier than a Friday. If I were in a better frame of mind, I would be excited by the buzz around the club. As it is, I'm nervous. What if Colt doesn't come? What if he decided that because I avoided him all week that it wouldn't be worth coming?

What if he does come? Will we talk? Do we come to terms that this wild attraction between us can't go anywhere? Or do we let go of logic for one night and do exactly what we want?

My mind is saying that I came here to get some form of closure, but my body knows better. I've silenced the rational side of my mind and let go of common sense. Even coming here was tempting the unrestrained, passionate parts of me. Parts that only spark to life when Colt is near.

I wander around the club and find the only other friendly face I know swinging. Tessa smiles and waves me over. I smile back and wave. The grumpy guy—Ransom, I think—is standing off to one side with his big arms crossed over his chest. He's watching the room, but even I can tell his focus is really on Tessa. His navy-blue shirt with a white band around the sleeve labels him as club security, but the way he's watching her makes me think there is a story there.

Tessa calls me over again. Just as I start to head her way, I catch sight of Colt. He's striding towards me with a single-minded purpose. I take two steps back, my eyes wide at the fierce look on his face.

He quickly closes the distance and tugs me into his arms. His lips landing on mine in a toe-curling kiss. I don't have time to think, let alone protest as he plunders, taking what he wants. There's no fight left in me. The moment his lips touch mine, I catch fire. I'm lost to our kiss, and the whole world fades away in our endless passion.

Colt lifts me from my feet, and I wrap my legs around him. Our lips don't part as he walks us away from the gathering crowd. I'm mildly aware that in this position, my bottom is likely on display. Again, I can't seem to worry about it. My butt cheeks are hardly the most scandalous thing this club will see tonight.

He kisses me with fierce possession all the way to one of the private rooms. The door slams shut behind us, and he twirls, pinning me to it. His cock presses firmly to my pussy as he rubs against me. My moans are swallowed by his mouth. His rough hands tug at the front of my dress, pulling it down until it's below my satin covered breasts.

With a low growl, he pushes my bra down too. My breasts are practically served up on a platter for him, and he takes full advantage. His fingers pluck at my nipples as his lips suck one tight bud into his mouth. I throw my head back against the door, moaning at the overwhelming sensations. I'm so turned on the littlest of touches could send me over the edge.

Colt must sense that because he pulls away, looking at me with those fathomless blue eyes. Eyes that tell me he wants to devour me, but that he's also furious and hasn't forgotten a minute of the time I've kept us apart. I can't hold in my whimper when he sets me down on the floor. Especially when my nipples rub over his shirt, sending shivers down my spine from their sensitivity.

"Darlene, fuck, babygirl," he growls. "I've needed to kiss you for days. Fucking days."

I nod, trying to catch my breath. The words escape me, but I can admit that I needed him too. This connection of ours won't be denied, and I was a fool for thinking it could be.

One night.

I can let go for one night, then put my self-control back in the driver's seat. I'm taking tonight for myself though. Nothing will stop me, not even the fact that it's a terrible idea.

"Me too... daddy?" I say the word like it's a question... what if he no longer wants me that way?

Colt makes a feral sound low in his throat. "Say it again, this time I want you to mean it."

"Daddy."

His lips crush to mine again until we're both breaking apart, panting for breath. With a groan of disappointment, he rights my bra and dress. "We need to talk, and I can't concentrate with these beauties teasing me."

He leads me to the rocking chair in the corner of the room. He sits then pulls me into his lap. I wriggle around a little, hoping that my ass on his cock will distract him, but he slaps my thigh in warning. I still instantly.

"Naughty girl."

I shrug. "I would say I'm sorry, but I'm not."

Colt chuckles, and I smile in return. He cups my cheek, and I sigh at the intimate contact, nuzzling into his touch. His fingertips skate down my neck then he's got his hand wrapped around the nape of my neck, keeping me still so he can look me directly in the eyes.

The way he's studying my expressions makes me feel exposed in a way I have never felt before.

"Tell me, why did you run from my office? Why have you been avoiding me?"

"Because you're my boss..."

"But I'm not. Not really. And there's no rule against us seeing each other."

He kisses me again, frying my brain cells and the protest that's on the tip of my tongue. Our lips part, and his tongue delves in. We kiss slow and sweet, completely opposite of our previous kisses but no less arousing.

This time it's me that pulls away. "What would the other faculty think, though? I'm new to the school. What kind of first impression will it make if I'm..." I wave my hands between us... "doing whatever this is."

"Who cares what they think. Let them talk."

I shake my head. "I don't want to get off on the wrong foot. This is my fresh start..."

He caresses my cheek, looking at me with tender softness. "What if I want to be part of that fresh start?"

"I-" I have to swallow around a lump in my throat. "I don't know..."

"Did you like what we did last Friday night?" he asks.

I blow out a breath and roll my eyes. "You know I did."

"Do you want to do that again?" He gives me a wolfish grin.

I shift on his lap, rubbing my thighs together. "Yes, daddy. But-"

"No buts," he growls. "You want to play, and so do I. In this room, we are just two consenting adults."

"What about outside this room?" I ask suspiciously.

"Outside this room—the club—we are co-workers. Maybe friends, if you want." He says it like it's the simplest, most cut and dry thing there is.

"I don't know if I can keep things separate like that..." I admit with a blush.

And it's true. Whenever I'm around him, my little side comes out to play. Even the few times I couldn't avoid him at school, I felt the instinct to defer to him... to let him lead the way. It's too tempting to give up my control to him. It's nothing like I've felt before for another person. It's not fair that the one person to bring that out in me is forbidden fruit.

"Darlene, we can be whatever you want us to be. I'm all in for whatever it is you decide. I want us to give this chemistry between us free reign, but I understand your reluctance, and in this one thing, I will let you lead the way."

Despite the fact that he wants more, I can tell he means every single word that he's said. It makes saying yes to things that much easier. I might change my mind when he's not right here touching me, but we can be together in the club and co-workers and friends outside of it. He's right that we are consenting adults. Sure, it might be complicated, but we can make it work...

I hope.

"Okay... we can try," I say cautiously. "I want to be your babygirl in private and co-workers at school."

The smile he gives me makes the decision worth it. It's hard to regret something when he's giving me that wolfish look. My insides clench, and my heart skips a beat. He looks both happy and hungry. I lick my lips, ready to relinquish control and let Colt lead the way.

"Good girl," he growls, his hand slowly running up and down my thigh, petting my skin gently. I shift in his lap as the heat grows between my legs. Every stroke of his fingers brings him closer to the apex of my thighs, where I need him the most. I shiver when he barely grazes the wet gusset of my panties, arousing me further. It's not enough. I need more—badly.

I whimper and wriggle myself closer to his hand, but he takes it away, not letting me seek out what I want. His other hand cups my breast, plumping and teasing over my clothes. He pinches my nipple, causing me to hiss out a breath, my core clenching, loving the bite of pain with the pleasure of being touched by him.

"Daddy..."

"Does my babygirl need something?"

"Yesss..." I hiss when he pinches my nipple harder, tugging on the sensitive bud.

He leans forward, gently licking and sucking at my neck—the sensations at complete opposites of the harsher touches to my breast. "What does my babygirl desire?" he growls against my skin.

"More..." I beg.

He chuckles lowly. "More what? Be specific."

My cheeks flush with shyness. I love being dirty talked to, but I've never been any good at it myself. But I'm so worked up and want him so badly that I'll do just about anything to please him. I want him so badly, I ache.

"I want you to touch me... m-my pussy," I stutter out. "My breasts."

His fingers trail up to my panties, stroking and rubbing me over the wet fabric. I throw my head back on a moan, wriggling my hips closer to the barely-there touch that's only making my need for him worse. He massages my breast over my dress, giving me exactly what I asked for and nothing more.

"Under my clothes..." I gasp as his touches continue to ramp up my lust. "T-touch my skin."

He stands me up in front of him and slowly unzips the back of my dress, letting it pool at my ankles. I stand before him in just my pink bra and panties. He lets out a growl of approval, kissing my stomach and up to the curve of my breasts over the top of my bra. He sucks my pale skin between his lips, sucking harder and harder until he leaves behind a bruise—marking me.

I've never liked that kind of thing. Hickies are something high school boys and girls do, not grown adults... but I love seeing his mark on me. I'm beginning to wonder what all I've been denying myself all these years, but I smash down that thought because I haven't denied myself. I've been waiting for someone like Colt to come and wrest that control away from me. To completely and utterly stake his claim. I mentally shake my head. No... I wasn't waiting for someone like Colt... I was waiting for Colt.

I can't imagine another man having the kind of power over my body like him. There's something about him that speaks directly to my base instincts. Whatever it is has my inner little ready to lay herself at his feet and do whatever he desires.

He stands in front of me, fully dressed in his suit and tie, looking proper and buttoned up but looking at me like a lion stalking his prey, and I'm the prey. I reach for him and push his jacket off his shoulders, and lay it over the arm of the chair. When I reach up for his tie, he grabs my wrists and shakes his head.

"I want to touch you," I say, letting my desires be known like he commanded.

"Not yet. I'm not done touching you, my beauty."

I flush at the praise. Have I ever been anyone's beauty? I haven't. I'm too curvy, too tall, always just too much of one thing or another. With Colt, I feel like his beauty. He makes me feel special. It's a heady feeling.

I shiver when his hands run over my shoulders, down my back to the clasp of my bra. Within a second, he has my bra undone, and it's on the floor with my dress. I gasp at the first touch of his big hands on my bare breasts. He hefts them in his hands, plumping them, then running his thumbs over my nipples.

My core clenches, and I feel like I might explode if he doesn't touch me. As if he can sense my need, he slips his hand into my panties and lightly strokes my core. His fingers slip between my wet lips and rub across my clit. My legs buckle, and I would melt to the floor without Colt's arm around my waist.

He walks me backward until my legs bump into the bed. Before I can sit, he turns me, and I find myself breathlessly over his lap, my bottom in the air.

"You didn't think it would be that easy, did you?" he asks with a growl. "You tried to run from me, naughty girl."

"But–"

"No buts. You should've talked to me. We could've figured things out sooner, and both of us would've been happier. Instead, you avoided me every chance you got and kept me on tenterhooks."

With a sigh, I grow slack over his lap, accepting his reprimand because he's not wrong. I earned this spanking. "I'm sorry, daddy," I say, meaning it.

"I understand why you avoided me, but avoidance is never the answer."

"I know. I really am sorry."

His hand caresses my bottom, tracing the edge of my panties, then pulling them down below my cheeks. "I think twenty-five... five for every day you avoided me."

I nod, ready to accept his punishment. I grip his leg, preparing for the upcoming barrage. The first several swats are a tease... I know he's warming me up. Preparing me for what's to come. The next five tell me how right I was as his hand cracks down harder and faster.

"Ow, daddy! It hurts!" I cry out.

"It wouldn't be a punishment if it didn't hurt."

His hand doesn't stop landing on my bottom. I lose count around sixteen, unable to concentrate on anything but the red-hot burn from my spanking. I yowl when his hand smacks down on my sit spots. Tears are flowing freely now, and my heart feels cracked wide open, waiting for him to crawl inside and stitch it back together—a terrifying concept.

Colt rubs my cheeks, massaging the abused flesh, both relieving and igniting the fire burning inside me. My pussy is slick with desire. My body a livewire waiting for him to flip the switch and give my body what it really needs.

"That's my good girl," he coos. "You took your spanking so well."

"I'm sorry, daddy..." I sniffle.

"And you're forgiven, beautiful girl."

He rights me on his lap, and I hiss out a breath at being sat upright on my flaming hot bottom. I wrap my arms around Colt's neck and snuggle into him. He pets my hair, rubbing my scalp and stroking his fingers through the strands. My tears dry up, and I relax against him, utterly replete.

I take a deep breath, then sit up, looking him in the eye. "Thank you, daddy. I didn't realize how badly I needed that."

His lips tip up in a smirk, his eyes crinkling slightly at the corners. "That's why I'm the daddy, and you're the sweet babygirl," he says, digging his fingers into my side, causing me to giggle.

I squirm on his lap until I feel the hard bar of his cock under me, then I'm wriggling for a totally different reason. All the desire from before comes rushing back to the surface, and I rub against him wantonly, begging with my body for what we both want. I squeal when he flips me over, laying me on the bed. My heart thuds in my chest at the shock of being moved so fast. Colt is so big and strong he can throw me around like a rag doll, and I love it.

I never thought I would like to be manhandled so much, but it's a fucking turn on. I always thought it would make me uncomfortable. I love my curves, don't get me wrong, but I've always worried that I'm too heavy to be carried around. Colt does it like I'm as light as a feather, and I love it.

He doesn't allow me to catch my breath before he's ripping my panties down my legs and licking at my soaked pussy. My back arches as he circles my clit with his wicked tongue.

"Daddy," I gasp at the sensation. I thread my fingers through his perfectly coiffed hair, messing it up. He laps and sucks at my clit, then moves lower, rimming my entrance before diving in with his tongue, fucking me with abandon.

He moves back up to my clit and sucks hard. I scream out my orgasm as it crashes through me like a tidal wave. My pussy clenches emptily, and I feel a moment of regret at Colt not being buried inside me as I come for him. I want to feel him deep while my release rips through me. I want to feel him come to completion with me.

CHAPTER SIX

Colt

SHE TASTES LIKE FUCKING HEAVEN. I could live and die by the taste of her sweetness. She arches, and her pussy floods my mouth with more of her sweet nectar. Darlene cries out as she's swept away with her release. She collapses back onto the mattress, and I crawl up her body, kissing her soft curves as I go, paying particular attention to her gorgeous breasts. I suck first one nipple, then the next.

Her fingers shuffle through my hair as she looks down at me with hooded eyes. I regretfully pull away, standing. She rises to her elbows and watches as I strip out of first my shirt, then my pants and boxers. She lets out a little gasp as my thick length springs free, her eyes growing wide as I stroke it.

I bend and grab a condom from my pants, tossing it to the bed beside Darlene before crawling between her legs. I go back to teasing her breasts, licking and nipping at her turgid nipples as my fingers find her slick heat. I slowly push two thick digits into her, fucking her with them. I scissor them, opening her up for me. Preparing her.

When she's moaning and moving her hips in time with my fingers, I roll the condom on my length and line myself up. I watch her eyes widen as I enter her for the first time. Her eyes fall closed, and her lips part on a moan.

"Fuck, baby, you're tight," I groan as her pussy stretches around my girth. I thought her pussy tasted like heaven. I was wrong. This is heaven. Burying my cock inside my beautiful babygirl is heaven, pure and simple.

My mouth finds her breast, and I suck and lap at her nipple, hungry for more of her sweet body. Her fingers fist in the sheets as she arches into my lips. I inch inside her slowly until I'm buried to the hilt. I pause there, giving her a chance to adjust to my thick length even though it's torture. Staying still inside her clenching heat is nearly impossible, but somehow, I manage to deny myself.

"Daddy... please," she whimpers, moving her hips to get the friction I'm denying us both.

I kiss her lips slowly, stroking her tongue with mine until her kiss turns hungry. Her tongue dances with mine, her teeth bite into my lower lip, nipping me. With a low growl, I pull out of her sweet heat, then inch back in.

Her hips punch up, swallowing up the last of my length in one harsh motion. Her legs wrap around me, her heels digging into my ass. "You won't break me," she says with a growl of frustration. "Fuck me, daddy."

I disentangle myself from her hold and flip her to her

hands and knees. Darlene gasps, then looks at me over her shoulder with heated eyes, daring me with a lick of her lips to take her exactly how I want. So I do. I grip her hips hard enough she'll be wearing my marks tomorrow and bury myself inside her in one hard thrust. She fists the sheets again as I lean over her body, gripping her shoulder and pulling her back into me with each thrust. She screams as I bottom out inside her pussy. The tight clench of her cunt has my balls drawing up and my spine-tingling, but I won't give in to my release—not yet.

I reach around her body, finding her swollen and needy clit. She moans, pushing herself back into my thrusts as I rub her sensitive button. "You're going to come on this cock while I fuck this naughty girl pussy.

"Yesss..." she hisses.

I slap her ass, and she cries out, her pussy locking down on my cock as her orgasm hits her like a freight train. I don't let up on her clit until she's collapsed on the bed in front of me, her ass still high in the air. I spank her again, bringing her release to new heights.

"Colt! Daddy!" Her head thrashes as she fists the bedding so hard her knuckles are white.

"That's it, beautiful..." I praise. "Let go. I've got you."

I fuck her straight through her orgasm and into another before I finally seek out my own climax. I pound into her tight sheath, fucking her so hard her ass bounces against my abs. I throw my head back on a roar as my come fills the condom. I have a brief moment of regret for the thin barrier. Something feral inside me wants to fill her up with me. Wants to mark her in the most primal way. I pull out, still in the throes of my climax, rip off the condom, and let the rest of my come splash on her ass. I rub my spend into the pink skin of her freshly spanked ass with my still hard cock, wanting back inside her but knowing she needs a reprieve.

I collapse to the bed beside her and pull her limp body into my arms. She cuddles into me, letting out a sigh as she catches her breath.

"That was..." she giggles lightly. "Beyond amazing."

I chuckle at her assessment, pressing a hard kiss to the top of her head. "It was."

Darlene snuggles closer, throwing one leg and one arm over my body, getting as close as she can. I hold her tighter, running my hand up and down her spine as we both come down from our high. She shivers, goosebumps rising on her skin. I pull the blanket over her body, and she instantly relaxes.

"Mm... thank you, daddy."

I kiss the top of her head once more. "You never have to thank me for taking care of you, beautiful."

"It's only polite to thank the man who just gave me the most satisfying sex of my life," she says, smiling against my chest.

I laugh. "Well, since we are being polite, I accept your thanks and return them."

She makes another humming noise as she drifts. I lie with her in my arms as she falls asleep, loving the warm weight of her against my body. She fits against me like she was made to be here. There's a part of me that feels like maybe she was made just for me. Everything inside me says that she's meant to be in my arms.

She's scared of what people will think, but with time, she'll realize that no one will judge her, nor will they care if we are together. In fact, most of the faculty will be happy for us. I've been at the school for ten years and have made a lot of friends among the staff. All of them will be pleased to see me happy, and in return, they will love her for bringing me that happiness.

Now to convince her. For now, I will allow her to think this is just a sordid interlude that we can turn on and turn off on a whim. She'll learn soon enough that it isn't what she really wants. I know she wants more, and I will be here waiting to give it all to her.

I'm not sure how much time passes before Darlene rouses. She sits up with a yawn, stretching her arms. "Sorry. I didn't mean to fall asleep on you."

I smirk. "No need to apologize. I love holding you."

Her cheeks heat with a blush. "Good thing I love being held."

"Mm... very."

We bask in each other for a few more minutes before we rise and dress. She giggles when she sees the mess we made of our clothes. "Seems like we will both be leaving a wrinkled mess."

I pull her into my arms and kiss her soundly. "You'll hear no complaints from me."

She pulls on her dress and shivers again. Not liking to see my girl cold, I put my suit jacket over her shoulders. She shrugs it on with a shy smile. "Thanks, daddy."

I kiss the tip of her nose. "What did I say about thanking me for taking care of you?"

She shrugs. "No idea," she says cheekily. "Guess you'll have to remind me."

I playfully slap her ass, and she giggles. Her smile

falls a few seconds later, and I pull her into my arms. "What's wrong, babygirl?"

She sighs. "Just sad this is over..."

I shake my head. "We aren't over. This isn't over. Not by a long shot. I agreed to explore this connection we have outside of school for your sake, but I refuse to let this be just one night. I think you feel the same..."

Darlene nods. "I can't imagine walking away," she admits.

I can hear the unspoken but in her tone. "But..."

She blows out a breath. "But I'm scared. I already feel so much... I don't know how it's possible to be," she waves her arms between us, "So connected like this after such a short time. It's scary."

With a knuckle under her chin, I tip her head up so she's looking me in the eyes. I want her to see the sincerity on my face when I give her my truth. "It is a little scary. Even I can admit that, but it scares me more to hide from the possibility of what this could be."

She chews her bottom lip but nods in agreement. "Yeah, I think so too. Just..."

"I know. You want to keep things to ourselves, and we will... for now," I qualify so she knows that hiding isn't something I want to do but something I'm doing for her peace of mind.

"For now," she agrees.

"Now, let's get out of here. There's a bath waiting with your name on it."

She gives me a confused look. "Where exactly are we going?"

"My house. If I only get the weekend with you, I want every minute I can get."

Surprisingly enough, she doesn't argue, just follows me to the parking lot and my truck. I help her in, and she asks about her car. I let her know we will get it tomorrow and that I'm not ready to have her out of my sight yet. She seems appeased by my statement. I have a feeling she doesn't want to be away from me either. It feels like the spell between us might break, and neither of us is prepared for that.

Thankfully it's a quick drive to my place because, within a couple minutes, Darlene is nodding off. By the time I pull into my garage, she's asleep. I lift her from the truck, and she sleepily wraps her arms around my neck. I carry her to the bedroom and lay her out on my bed before going to the bathroom and running her a bath.

She whines that she's tired when I strip her from her clothes, but she moans contentedly when I put her in the hot water of the bath. She sinks into the bubbles happily, laying her head back on the lip of the tub. I carefully wash her clean, taking my time to massage out any tension in her muscles. She's nothing but a pliant, wet woman when I finish. Her eyes are half-closed when I lift her from the tub and dry her.

I once again carry her to bed and pull back the blankets. She crawls in without a single protest. I strip and take a quick shower, then wrap my body around hers, letting sleep take me.

WHEN I WAKE UP, Darlene is still fast asleep. I carefully disentangle her from around me and pull on a pair of gray sweatpants. I quietly close the bedroom door and start making breakfast. I'm flipping the last pancake when I hear the bedroom door open. She walks into the kitchen, wearing one of my shirts, and my dick is instantly hard.

Fuck she looks like sin in my clothes. I want to rip my t-shirt off her body and fuck her right here on the counter, breakfast be damned. She closes the distance between us, and I'm slightly shocked that she wraps her arms around my middle and hugs me to her curvy frame. I return the hug, pulling her close. She tilts her face up and looks at me with a sultry smile.

"Morning, daddy."

I press my lips to hers, giving her a brief kiss. She tries to deepen it, but I pull away, knowing that if I kiss her any more than a quick peck, I'll have her pinned to the counter fucking her like my cock wants.

"Good morning, sleeping beauty. Did you sleep well?"

"Mm... very."

I press another quick kiss to her lips. "Good. I made breakfast."

She peeks around me and smiles when she sees the pile of pancakes and bacon. "My favorite! How'd you know?"

I chuckle. "Good guess. What little girl doesn't like pancakes? And it takes a monster to not like bacon. And you're no monster."

Darlene lets out a little growl. "I could be a monster," she says playfully, nipping at my shoulder.

"My fierce little monster. I do apologize."

She laughs a full belly laugh. "You're forgiven for the oversight. Thank goodness this monster loves bacon."

I make her a plate and pour her a glass of juice. I set her place at the table, but when I sit down, she crawls into my lap instead. My cock throbs under her ass as she wriggles into a comfortable position.

I laugh when she pushes my plate to the side and pulls hers into place. "Comfortable?"

She turns and smirks at me, giving her bottom another little wiggle. "Very," she says, then tucks into her food.

After breakfast, we both take a quick shower and make plans for the day. Since she's new to the city, I decide to take her to the art museum. She wanders from painting to painting, getting more excited as she goes.

"Look at this one!" she says animatedly. "The colors and the brush strokes... You can practically feel what the artist felt when he painted it. I can feel his yearning for the woman in the painting. He must've loved her very much."

I make a humming sound in agreement, thinking I'm starting to know how he felt because even though it's been such a short time since I met Darlene, she's already asserted herself into my heart. I can't imagine a life without her in it. I should be scared at feeling this depth of emotion so quickly, but I can't seem to find the fear. I feel nothing but excitement and desire.

I follow her through the whole museum, loving her enthusiasm. She shares her thoughts on just about every painting, even the ones she doesn't like. I love how happy she is, and it pleases me that I was able to do this with her. Seeing her in her element is a sight to behold for sure. I can't wait to see her work. I can tell just from her excitement that she's got a great eye, and

I can imagine how brilliantly that translates to her own art.

After the museum, I regretfully take her to her car. I offer her dinner, but she declines, saying she really needs to work on her curriculum for the week. Wanting to prove to her that I respect her time and her dedication to her career, I don't argue. I simply kiss her silly and help her into her car. She drives off with a little wave, and I feel like I'm watching a piece of my heart drive away.

CHAPTER SEVEN
Darlene

MONDAY MORNING COMES EARLIER than I wanted. I tossed and turned half the night last night. How is it that after just one night in Colt's bed, I feel like my own bed is inadequate? I missed his arms wrapped around me and the warmth of his body against mine. All feelings that tell me I'm in big trouble when it comes to keeping him at arm's length outside of the club.

The school is quiet when I get there. I came early to get my room prepared for my first class—a lecture on art history. I set up the prints of the Mona Lisa and Starry Night—two of my favorite paintings.

I'm writing notes on the whiteboard when a voice behind me startles me. "Good morning!"

I quickly turn, holding my hand to my heart at the scare. A portly man with a balding head stands in the doorway to my classroom. He's wearing a plaid flannel shirt that's tucked into a pair of slacks that are at least an inch too short for his stature. I force a smile to my face, not liking the way his eyes boldly trail up and down my body.

"Sorry, I didn't mean to startle you," he says with fake chagrin. "I didn't get the chance to introduce myself last week."

He walks across the room, his hand outstretched. I put my hand in his clammy one as he gives me a limp handshake. "I'm Levi Troy. I teach science."

"Darlene Larson. Nice to meet you, Mr. Troy."

He clicks his tongue. "Now, we don't have to be so formal. Call me Levi."

I give him a half-hearted nod, not wanting to be anything but formal with this man. Something about him has my creeper radar going off something fierce. Thankfully the first bell rings, and students start flooding into the room.

"Well, I better get to class to keep these idiots in line."

I narrow my eyes and give him a disgusted look. How could a teacher think that his students are idiots? Why even become a teacher if you dislike kids? I shake my head without commenting. Thankfully he leaves quickly, and I don't have to come up with any kind of response.

"Okay, class, settle down..."

The morning passes by in a blur, and before I know it, it's lunchtime. The teacher's lounge is nearly empty, aside from three other teachers whom I met last week. "Darlene!" Patty says with genuine enthusiasm. "How's your second week going so far?"

"So far, so good. The students have all been well behaved after the little incident last week."

Coach Lockwood chuckles. "I can imagine so. Todd and Leon aren't enjoying their punishment very much and have warned the entire student body not to mess with you."

I shake my head with a smirk. "Well, I guess it's better to start off the semester with them afraid that I'm going to send them to Principal James than have them try to run roughshod all over me."

Patty laughs, "Darn straight. There are some great kids here, but they definitely need to know who is boss. Some of them can get rowdy if they aren't put in their place quickly."

"She definitely did that," a familiar voice says from behind me.

I turn and see Colt striding into the breakroom. He goes to the fridge and pulls out a dish, then warms it in the microwave. I look at our small table, seeing that the only empty chair is directly beside me. My body heats, and I can feel my nipples pebble beneath my shirt. I thank God that I'm wearing the matching jacket to my skirt; it does the job of hiding my instant attraction to Colt.

A small part of me hopes that he's going to take his lunch back to his office because surely there is no way that I can hide the desire to touch him every time he's near. A larger, greedy part of me wants him to sit next to me. To walk up and claim my lips and mark me as his right here in front of everyone. I push that part of me down because that's crazy. It's the exact opposite of what I want him to do.

He sits down, and nothing happens. I don't self-combust. I don't throw myself at him and kiss him like crazy. He just sits beside me with a benign smile, the same smile he gives the rest of the teachers. My heart clenches, and I hate it even though it's exactly what I asked for.

"So what did you do this weekend, Miss Larson?" Colt asks. "Stayed out of trouble, I hope."

I choke on the sip of water I just took at his question. His big hand is instantly on my back, rubbing and patting as I cough. He gives me a worried, but knowing look. I clear my throat, trying to get my bearings.

"My weekend was okay. I went to the art museum. Nothing exciting," I say with a smirk just for him.

"Oh really?" he says, returning my smirk with a sly grin of his own.

"Yep."

"You really should check out the downtown historical museum if you like museums; it's amazing," Patty says with enthusiasm.

"Or the aquarium," Melinda says quietly. "I love going there." She blushes bright red when she realizes that she's gathered the attention of all of us. I've noticed in the short time that I've known Melinda that she's incredibly soft-spoken and shy around her colleagues, but in front of her class, she's loud and in charge. A total juxtaposition if ever there was one.

"Oh, I love aquariums," I say excitedly.

I look at Colt, and he smiles at me, giving me an imperceptible nod, which tells me he's making a note of it. Excitement courses through me at the thought of spending another day with him. I jump in my seat when his hand surreptitiously rests on my thigh under the table. He lightly squeezes, and I barely bite back my moan at the forbidden touch.

Outwardly, he's being a perfect gentleman, following the rules I set for him. Keeping our secret. Inwardly, he's obviously struggling with the confines enough to bend the rules. I put my hand on top of his, giving him a warning squeeze. His hand turns, and he threads his fingers through mine, briefly squeezing them before releasing me.

That small connection cements my knowledge that I'm in deep with Colton James. He's going to steal my heart, and I'll just have to hope that he'll be careful with it.

The rest of the day moves slower than the first half. My kids are good but getting them to focus on their projects is like herding cats with a water hose. Impossible. I'm cleaning up for the day when there is a rap on the doorframe. I turn with a smile, suspecting it's Colt... I'm disappointed when I realize it's Levi.

"Come to dinner with me," he asks without any preamble. Though saying he asked is a bit of a stretch since he actually demanded it.

I try to smile, but I have a feeling the look on my face reads more like disgust than friendly. "Sorry, I've already got plans tonight."

Like scrubbing toilets with my toothbrush, I think to myself. Something that is much more appealing than going anywhere with him.

He tsks. "Tomorrow then."

I shake my head. "I don't date co-workers," I say with fake sadness.

"Who said it had to be a date," he says with a raise of his bushy eyebrows. He licks his dry lips and looks me up and down in a slimy way that makes my skin crawl. "Just a little fun between colleagues."

"Sorry... I don't do that either."

There is a soft knock on the door, and Melinda comes in. "Are you ready?" she asks shyly, coming to my rescue.

I give her a grateful smile and grab my things. "Yes, I'm starving!"

I follow her out to the parking lot, and she turns, looking back at the building with disgust. "Sorry for stepping in back there..."

"No, thank you for stepping in, seriously. Dinner is on me tonight," I say with a smile.

"Oh," she says with wide eyes. "I didn't mean... you don't have to..."

I give her a kind smile. "I want to. It's the least I can do for you being my knight in shining armor."

That gets a real laugh from her. "Mr. Troy is a real piece of work. Definitely avoid him if you can."

"That's my new goal in life," I agree. "Now, how about pizza? I think we deserve something nice and greasy after that."

Melinda gives me the scoop on all of the teachers as we eat. I notice she mentions Coach Lockwood several times, and if I'm not mistaken, it's with a dreamy smile on her face. I'm guessing there's something there, even if she doesn't know it yet. The way he looked at her at lunch made it seem like he was ready to eat her for lunch instead of his food.

"Principal James is a whole other thing altogether,"

Melinda says, taking a bite of her pizza. She chews so slowly I could strangle her for leaving me hanging.

"What about Principal James?" I somehow manage to keep my tone calm and collected when, in reality, I'm chomping at the bit for any little piece of information she might divulge.

"Well, first of all, he's got the whole silver fox thing going for him. All the single female staffers want him, but he doesn't pay them the time of day. He's respectful of his position at the school." She shrugs. "I mean, I don't see the draw, but everyone else seems to go gaga when they are around him."

"Huh..." I can't seem to come up with a better response as jealousy courses through me at the idea of dozens of women throwing themselves at my daddy.

Oh crap. Did I just stake a claim on Colt? I think I did. Which means I'm already in deep with him. I really do want more than just weekends at the club. I should be freaking out, but I'm not. The only thing I feel is desire for him. In fact, I'm kicking myself for not getting his phone number. Maybe I could stop by his place? Would that be terribly forward of me? He's the one who was upfront about wanting more than just time at the club.

I push those thoughts aside and enjoy the rest of my meal with my new friend. I can worry about the rest later. For now, I'm going to relax and eat my greasy pizza and laugh about the time Coach Lockwood dressed down the entire marching band for groaning over doing halftime in the rain, then promptly slipped on the wet grass, nearly falling to his butt.

CHAPTER EIGHT

Colt

I stay at the school longer than normal doing paperwork and sending emails. People don't realize how much work being the principal of a school can be. It's not all punishing students for being bad and making sure that the teachers are on track with their curriculums. Once I've fully caught up on everything, and there isn't a single thing left to do, I decide to head to the gym and get in a workout.

One of the perks of working at Thurston Academy is the top-notch gym on-site that I have twenty-four-hour access to as the principal. I'm not surprised to see Cooper lifting weights. He might be an ex-football player, but he hasn't let himself go soft now that he's a high school gym coach. No, he's as fit as he was when he played for Pittsburg all those years ago.

"Hey, Coop," I greet, walking to the treadmill for my warmup.

"You're here late."

"I had a shit ton of paperwork to catch up on and

decided to work out my frustration before heading home." By frustration, I mean sexual frustration. I love my job and all that it entails... it's the sexual tension and the desire to head straight for Darlene's apartment once I leave here that I need to work out of my system.

I set the treadmill to a faster pace than my standard warmup, starting at a flat outrun. After a few minutes, I up the speed until my mind is cleared of everything except my muscles' stretch and pull as my feet rise and fall.

I'm sweating profusely by the time I finally slow the speed for my cooldown. I move on to weights and realize that I'm alone. Cooper must've noticed that I wasn't good company and gave me the privacy I obviously needed.

I lift until my muscles burn, but my need to be near Darlene hasn't eased at all. Just that innocent touch under the lunch table today was enough to drive me insane. I shower off and head home. Barely keeping my steadfast resolve to stay away from her as I turn the opposite direction of her home.

I make it ten minutes before texting her, and I'm honestly surprised I lasted that long.

CHAPTER NINE
Darlene

My phone pings on my way home, and I wonder who it is. No one here has my number and Charity would still be at cheer practice so it can't be her. I wait until I'm inside my apartment to check it. I pull out my phone and see the text is from 'daddy.'

Thinking about you, is all it says.

I smile, not even upset that at some point this weekend he managed to add his phone number into my contacts without me knowing. I kick off my shoes and put on some cozy clothes before responding. My mind going over dozens of things to say, but only one thing keeps running through my mind... how much I miss him.

I miss you, daddy.

No sooner than I've sent the message, my phone rings. My heart skips a beat, and a warm lightness spreads through my body.

"Hello," I greet.

"Hi, babygirl. I don't like you missing me when we could be together," he growls.

I know how he feels, which is the only explanation for my next words. "You could always come see me," I offer, feeling bold.

"What about the rules?" he asks warily as if he doesn't trust that I know what I'm asking for.

I do. Even though I'm skating a fine line between keeping things casual and at the club or at the very least keeping our relationship out of the weekday grind, I can't seem to find it in me to care. I'm realizing that just because it's a school night doesn't mean we can't be together. We're not at work, and no one will know. Why deny ourselves?

Right?

"Seeing you on a weekday isn't against the rules as long as we are professionals at work. Anything goes on our off hours..."

"Anything?" he growls possessively.

"Why don't you come over and find out?" I tease.

I give him my address, though I have a feeling he already knows it. He promises to see me soon, and we hang up. I look around my apartment. Crap. I should have asked to go to his place. Mine looks like I haven't been living here for three weeks. I haven't even started unpacking the living room, and my kitchen looks like I'm living out of boxes—because I am.

Twenty minutes later, there is a knock on my door. I open it to find Colt looking sexy as heck in a pair of dark wash jeans and a t-shirt that's stretched tight across his broad shoulders and chest. I lick my lips taking him in. It's the most casual I've seen him except for his sweatpants at his house yesterday morning.

He looks darn sexy in his buttoned-up suits, but he is a sight to behold in casual jeans and a fitted t-shirt.

"Are you going to invite me in?" he asks with a chuckle.

"Oh, yes..." I stutter, "Yes, come in. Sorry."

"No need to apologize. I like that you enjoy what you see."

I blush hotly and step aside, inviting him in. He takes in my place with a frown.

"Sorry, it's kind of a mess. I wasn't thinking when I invited you," I say, feeling silly for having a visitor—especially Colt—with my home looking so messy and not put together.

"Why haven't you unpacked yet?" he asks, looking at the piles of boxes.

I shrug. "I've been distracted... and I hate unpacking. Well, packing too... really the whole moving process stinks. I did unpack my bathroom and my studio," I say proudly.

Colt smirks and comes closer to me until I can feel the heat of his body. I instantly come alive, desperate for his touch. My body sways towards him, wanting to close that small distance between us. Wanting to touch and be touched. Everything inside me sings whenever he's near.

Just like at lunch today, my body responds. My nipples pebble, and my pussy heats. Just being close has me wanton and needy.

I clutch his shirt in my fists, tipping my head back and closing my eyes as I wordlessly ask for a kiss. He doesn't leave me wanting. Colt cups my cheeks in his big hands, caressing me with his thumbs as his lips land on mine in a soul-searing kiss.

Our lips move together like we've kissed a million times before. His hands gently hold me to him as if I might disappear if he doesn't. What he doesn't realize is that I'm not going anywhere. My lips part, and Colt deepens our kiss. Our tongues dance together with him leading the way. I completely lose myself in him. The kiss goes on forever, and yet, not nearly long enough.

He pulls his lips from mine, and I gasp for breath. His arms wrap around me, holding me close. I positively melt into him, feeling content and cherished for the first time ever. No one has ever made me feel the way Colt does. He fills a hole I didn't even realize was inside me. I should be freaked out—and to some extent, I am, but I also feel elated.

"Better now?" he quietly asks.

"Mm... much, daddy. I'm glad you're here."

He kisses the top of my head. "Good. I'm glad."

He holds me for a long time, and it feels fantastic to be wrapped up in him. When he finally releases me, I feel centered in a way that only comes with a good spanking. That's another thing that should scare me about this thing with Colt. It's too soon to be feeling so much... isn't it? I shake the thought off and pull him further into my apartment and give him a tour.

"Well, this is the living room and kitchen... obviously. I lead him down the hallway pointing to the bathroom and my bedroom. I bypass the studio, not sure that I want him to see what I've been working on lately, considering how often he's shown up in my work recently.

"Is this your studio?" he asks, indicating the only closed door. He gives me a quizzical look and asks if he can see it. I chew on my bottom lip nervously but nod. I open the door and let him enter ahead of me.

He grunts when he sees the room for the first time, and my lip gets another bit of abuse from my teeth as I bite down on it to keep myself from asking him what he's thinking. I choke back my words. I don't want praise for my art. I'm confident that the paintings and sketches are good. It's the wanting to know if he's freaked out that I have half a dozen pieces that are nothing but him.

Colt turns and looks at me with an unreadable expression. "You did all these?"

I nod, unable to form words.

"These are..." he starts but stops and walks to the big painting in the center of the room that's my favorite. The only thing I can't seem to get right is the exact icy blue of his eyes... other than that, it's perfectly him. "They're amazing. I can't believe you did this. Why me?"

I laugh. "Isn't it a bit obvious?" I ask. "It seems like I'm a little obsessed with you. I promise it's not in a creepy way. I just can't seem to get you out of my head and whenever something is stuck in my mind," I wave my hands around the room, indicating the images of him on the walls and easels, "it comes out in my art."

He sweeps me off my feet and kisses me with a fierce ownership. I don't question it. I wrap my legs around his waist and kiss him back just as ferociously. My back hits the wall, and I groan. Colt thrusts up against my aching pussy. My eyes roll back in my head at the sensation. Not just the physical, but the heady feeling of him wanting me so much too.

It's intoxicating.

His hands tug at my shirt, and mine are tugging at his. Then we are skin on skin, and it's everything. My bra falls away, and his chest hair abrades my hard nipples shooting pleasure straight to my core. Our kiss intensifies, then slows, turning into something softer... gentler. He kisses me like I'm something precious. Something that deserves to be treasured.

With a hand under my butt and one threaded through my hair, he carries me to the bedroom, never once lifting his lips from mine. I slide down his body, he holds me close, tilting my head just so to deepen our kiss even further. Our tongues dance and twirl. I reach for his jeans, quickly undoing his belt and unzipping them. I put my hand inside, rubbing his hard length behind the soft cotton of his underwear.

Colt groans into my lips, telling me how good my touch feels. With reluctance, he pulls away from my hand. "Not yet, babygirl."

I whimper, not liking being denied. "I want to make you feel good, daddy."

He lowers his lips to my nipple, licking the tight peak. "You do make me feel good," he growls against my flesh.

He nips the sensitive bud, and it's my turn to groan at the lust-inducing feeling. That little bit of pain amps up my desire, bringing my wanton self to the forefront. I thread my fingers through his hair, messing up his perfectly styled locks. Colt falls to his knees in front of me and slowly works my yoga pants and panties down my legs. I step out of them, now completely bared to him.

If it weren't for the look of hunger on his face, I

might feel self-conscious about being naked with him on his knees in front of me. He's at perfect eye level to see all of my least favorite parts of my body, but the way he's looking at me makes it impossible to listen to any of those insecurities.

Colt taps one of my ankles, soundlessly telling me to open my legs for him. I widen my stance and watch as he leans in, kissing the top of my mound. He kisses lower until his lips are directly over my sensitive clit. He lightly kisses the bundle of nerves sending waves of need coursing through me. My knees buckle as his touch overwhelms my senses.

"Lay back on the bed, beauty."

I do as he says, letting him take the lead. My heart beats an uneven staccato at how easily I surrender to his every whim. Trust doesn't come easily for me, and already I trust this man to take care of me and not abuse his power.

I lie on the bed, waiting for whatever Colt is going to do next. I watch as he discards his jeans and underwear, leaving him completely naked in front of me. I eat up the image he makes. He's tall with broad shoulders and sculpted muscles that trail down his abdomen to the thick length that's standing proudly against his lower stomach. I lick my lips at the sight of his needy cock.

I only get a brief moment to enjoy him before he's kneeling between my thighs and kissing me. His lips don't linger at mine, despite my trying to hold him to me. He instead kisses down my jaw, lightly nipping the place on my neck where my pulse thrums before working his way down to my breasts. He spends time licking and sucking at each nipple. My pussy floods with arousal, desperate for his touch.

His rough hands rub up and down my belly, cupping my breasts then moving lower until his fingers are slipping through my folds, finding me hot and wet.

"Fuck, babygirl, you're drenched."

I nod quickly. "For you, always."

He growls low in his throat, a feral sound if ever there was one. "Only for me."

"Yes," I moan as he thrusts one thick digit deep inside my needy pussy. I whimper when he kisses his way down my body and to my clit. He takes it between his lips and lashes it with his tongue—my back arches at the intensity. The fingers of one hand pluck my nipple while the other thrusts deep inside my core, finding my g-spot with every motion.

It doesn't take long before my body seizes up in an earth-quaking orgasm. "That's it. Come all over my fingers. Let me lick up your sweet cream."

As if I could hold back. My thighs squeeze around his head, and he pushes them open wider, keeping me from controlling any part of his glorious assault against my senses. He sucks my clit between his teeth, nipping the oversensitive bundle of nerves until I'm screaming. My pussy clenches hard around his fingers.

He wrings every bit of release from my body until I'm limp on the bed, spread out for his pleasure. I watch him lick his lips, then clean his fingers with his mouth before crawling up my body and resting his hard cock at the apex of my thighs. He reaches for the condom I didn't realize he produced from his pants pocket.

"I'm on the pill," I say before he can roll the condom down his length. "And I'm clean."

He groans and tosses the condom aside. "I'm clean... fuck baby, are you sure?"

I move my hips, rubbing my wetness over his thick cock. "Yes. Make love to me, daddy. I want to feel you... all of you."

He takes me at my word and slowly starts to enter me. He feels like heaven inside me. He doesn't just slam into me; he slowly breaches my entrance... sliding each inch inside me in an achingly slow stroke.

"You feel so fucking good, Darlene. Like a little piece of heaven sent down just for me."

Colt buries himself deep and I groan at the sharpness of the feeling of him pressed so firmly against the end of me. Never has a man filled me so completely—my core aches in the best way. I roll my hips, wrapping my legs around him to hold him tight to me.

"Please, daddy..."

With aching slowness, he retreats until just the tip of him is perched at my entrance, then he thrusts forward, slow and steady. I claw at his back, urging him on. His control doesn't waver though. No, he builds a slow but hard pace, burying himself deep with every thrust.

"Yesss..." I hiss, raking my nails over his shoulders as I pull him down for a kiss. Our bodies move in perfect sync as we make love. Slow and hard. Heat builds gradually in my core. My orgasm is slowly being pulled out from my depths. Each stroke against my g-spot makes me see stars. Before long, my climax is crashing through me, and I'm screaming Colt's name. He kisses away my noises. Fireworks explode before my eyes, and I'm temporarily blinded by the light and heat that's engulfing me.

"Look at me," Colt demands.

I pry my eyes open, meeting his fierce blue gaze as he works me through my orgasm. He quickens his pace, driving my pleasure higher until I'm crying out again. Colt grinds against my clit and even though my eyes want to fall closed, I keep them on him. Watching as his own pleasure grows to a crescendo.

"Gonna fill this pussy so good, babygirl."

"Come in me, daddy. Fill me up," I beg. "I want to feel it. Feel you."

My dirty words are all it takes for him to lose control. He pounds into my pussy, chasing his own release. I watch as he stares straight through me, his cock pulsing inside me as his release overcomes him. I feel his warmth fill me and spill out between us. The dirtiness of it triggers another, smaller orgasm from me. I collapse under him completely and utterly replete.

He leans in and kisses me soft and sweet before moving beside me on the bed and pulling me against his chest. We're quiet as our breathing evens out and our hearts stop pounding. I snuggle deep inside the circle of his arms, loving how good it feels to be held. My eyes fall closed, and drowsiness pulls me under into a restful sleep.

The next morning, I wake up in a panic when I realize my alarm didn't go off. Strong arms flex around me, and I relax. "It's only five, babygirl, relax." My alarm didn't go off because it's not even time to wake up yet. I doze for the next half hour cuddled against Colt's strong body.

When my alarm does go off, I lightly kiss his chest before turning it off. "You stayed."

He gives me a sexy, sleepy smile. "I stayed."

"What about work?" I ask, chewing my lip nervously. If we leave at the same time people will see us arrive together... People will talk.

"What about it?" he asks, confused.

"Well, you're here... first of all, you don't have anything to wear. Secondly, we can't show up at the same time. This is bad..."

He shakes his head, stands from the bed in all his naked glory. My mouth goes dry at seeing him in the light of day. His toned muscles flex as he walks out of the room. My eyes gravitate towards his ass and what a sexy ass it is. I lick my lips, wanting to take a bite out of it. He comes back into the room carrying a bag. I didn't notice last night.

Hell, I barely notice it right now. Now that he's facing me, I'm drooling for another reason. His cock is hard and standing proudly against his lower abs. I prowl towards him, licking my lips hungrily. Colt lets out a low growl and stalks toward me. His hand grips the back of my head, pulling me into him for a searing kiss. I grind against his length, loving the feel of his hardness against my softness.

I reach between us and grip his cock giving it a teasing stroke. "Fuck, babygirl."

I move away from him, taking a step towards the bathroom. "We're going to be late..."

He growls, following my retreat. "Then I guess we better take a shower." He picks me up and tosses me over his shoulder, his hand cracking down on my upturned bottom. I giggle at his playfulness. The worries over him staying the night and us potentially getting caught together fading away.

When we're alone together, my worries seem far away, and I just feel happy—a ridiculous amount of happiness. I forget to be scared that our relationship has gone from zero to sixty and just concentrate on the time we are together. There will be time to worry about reality later. Right now, there is a naked man in my shower with me, and that's the only thing that matters.

CHAPTER TEN

Colt

"We can't show up together," Darlene argues. The sweet pliable woman from our shared shower is gone. In her place is someone wrought with nervousness.

"Beauty, no one is going to care if we are together," I argue. "They will be happy for us." No matter how many times I repeat myself, she doesn't seem to listen.

"You don't know that for sure," she accuses. "You don't understand how it'll look for the new girl to be dating the man in charge."

I shake my head, not liking how upset she's getting. "Okay, okay, babygirl. We will do this your way."

Her shoulders fall, and she puffs out a deep breath releasing some of the anxiety that was building to a crescendo. "Thank you," she says with noticeable relief.

I'm not sure why she's got it in her head that anyone will judge her for our relationship, but I'm determined to get to the bottom of it. Only once we get past that hurdle can we move forward beyond what we have now.

For now, this will have to be enough. I don't want to push her too hard and too fast.

We're already moving at lightning speed. In time she will realize how silly it is to hide our relationship.

"I'll go in first since I usually drive, and you can walk like normal. How does that sound?"

She gives me a bright smile and nods. "Yes, that's good. No one will suspect anything."

We walk to the front of her building together where I give her a scorching kiss before leaving her on the front steps and going to my car. I can't help shaking my head at my woman walking in one of her prim skirts with her coat done up tight to fight away the chill in the morning air. She could be warm in the car beside me if she weren't so damn stubborn.

The school is already a livewire of activity when I pull into my parking space. Several of the students wave or stop me to talk to me about one of the many extracurriculars I take part in running here at school. When other schools are defunding the arts program and extracurricular activities, Thurston Academy is proudly adding funding to help promote creative development.

"Morning, Colt," Judy says with a smile. "How are you today?"

I return her infectious smile. That's one thing about the office administrator that I've always loved. She's almost always smiling and happy to help. "I'm good, Judy. How are you?"

"Oh, good, good, you know me. I've got some messages for you from the answering service," she grumbles as much as her perkiness will allow, handing me the slips of paper.

I leaf through them quickly and chuckle at seeing Leon and Todd's parents' names on the top two messages. Apparently, they aren't happy that their sons are benched for the next couple games. Too damn bad. No one disrespects any of my staff the way they disrespected Darlene... especially not Darlene.

"Thanks, Judy," I say, heading into my office to make a couple phone calls.

I EAT my lunch in my office, knowing that I won't be able to control myself if Darlene is within touching distance. It's almost impossible to push down the urge to claim her in front of everyone. I want people to know that she's mine. Especially since I heard from Coop that Mr. Troy has been sniffing around her and that it might be a problem.

We've been suspicious of him since the second teacher quit without notice or warning. When the third teacher quit, it became apparent that there was a problem and that Mr. Troy could be the cause. Unfortunately, we have yet to be able to prove the sexual harassment we suspect him of, and none of the teachers wanted to discuss why they decided to quit.

A quick look at the clock shows me that Darlene is on her free hour. The temptation to see her is too much to resist any longer. I stride to her classroom with a single-minded focus... getting her soft lips under my own. Seeing that Darlene is alone in her classroom, I close the door and lower the blind over the little window.

With a low growl, I close the distance between us. Darlene holds her hands out to stop me, but I refuse to be denied. I grip her wrists and pin her arms behind her back.

"What are you doing?" she asks, breathless.

"Isn't it obvious?"

She licks her lips, teasing me with her pink tongue. Yeah, she knows exactly what she's doing to me. I lean in and press my lips to hers in a chaste kiss. Just like I knew she would, she arches against me, pulling at her wrists. When she responds to my kiss, moving her lips with mine, I release her hands. They instantly move to my chest, gripping my shirt in both fists as she returns my passion.

I break our kiss, heaving in a breath. "I can't stay away. Knowing you're just down the hall, unkissed by me, is driving me insane," I growl, pulling her closer and kissing her sweet lips again.

She completely surrenders to the onslaught. Kissing me back with everything she is. Her fingers fisted in my shirt as our passion grows. I cup her breast over her shirt, rubbing my thumb over her hardened nipple. She moans into my lips as I tease her. When the bell rings, I reluctantly pull away, knowing that it's only a matter of minutes before students start pouring in.

"Come to the club with me tonight." It's not really a question, and she knows it. She'd be right because the only answer is yes. I won't take no for an answer, not when I want her so badly.

"Yes," she responds, not even hesitating or arguing that it's a school night.

"Pick you up at seven."

Her fingers touch her well-kissed lips. "Okay, Colt. See you then."

CHAPTER ELEVEN
Darlene

I TAKE one last look at myself in the mirror and decide my outfit is perfect. A mint green dress with peek-a-boo lace cutouts. It's not like most of my club dresses, it's a bit on the sexier side, but the frilly skirt and little green bow right between my breasts make the dress a nice mix between the two.

There is a knock at my door at seven sharp. I love that Colt isn't one to be late. I love that he's as excited as I am for a night together. It's not the weekend. I know that, but staying away is not something I'm going to be able to do. I didn't even have the willpower to keep him from kissing me today at school.

Part of me wants to say to hell with it and just come out in the open with our relationship, but the other part is scared about what others will think still. I want to wait and see where this thing is going with Colt before we go public. We've only known each other for such a short time... what if he bores of me? Or what if our connection isn't as strong as I think it is?

Excuses. Both of them because I know that our chemistry isn't something that will just disappear, and it's not something that will falter or fizzle. I've never felt the kind of chemistry that I do with him, and I just have a feeling only good things will come from it. I just need to be one-hundred percent sure before we become public.

I open the door with a huge smile. Colt returns my smile, looking me up and down like he wants to eat me up. "You look amazing, babygirl."

I feel my cheeks heat with an uncharacteristic blush. That's another thing that Colt brings out in me—shyness. I've always been bold—even with my little side—but I'm different with Colt. It's like my little side hasn't ever fully come to the surface, and Colt coaxes it out of me. I love it. I love feeling completely free of any constraints.

"Thank you, daddy."

"Are you ready?"

"Yes, daddy," I nod excitedly.

He wraps an arm around me, reeling me into his body and kissing me. "We could always stay in if you'd prefer..."

I scrunch up my nose. "After getting all dressed up?"

He taps my nose. "Good point. Let's go, babygirl."

The club is busier than I thought it would be on a weeknight. Colt explains that because it's such a small and close-knit community that the club tends to be full most nights. He also points out that with the restaurant, it's a popular date night spot as well.

"Did you eat?" he asks.

I chew on my bottom lip, thinking about the half a

bowl of dry cereal I munched on while getting ready. "Yes?"

"Is that an answer or a question?"

"Well... see... I was so excited and nervous that I kind of only ate a little cereal."

Colt smirks and gives me a tender look. "You never have to be nervous to spend time with me, beauty. I will take the excited any time, but you also need to eat. Let's go get dinner," he says, guiding me to the entrance to the restaurant.

We're seated right away. Colt is stopped by several people on the way to our table. It seems like everyone here knows and respects him. I have a sense of pride that this wonderful man has picked me to be at his side.

"Your waitress will be with you shortly," the maître d' says as we take our seats.

"Thanks, Richard," Colt says with a smile.

I look at the menu, pleasantly surprised to see that it —like the bar—is set up for both littles and dominants. The only problem, I'm overwhelmed with how many options there are. I consider the salmon, but it comes with brussels sprouts, which's never a good thing. The chicken tenders sound good but could be seen as a childish choice. What if Colt doesn't want little me right now? The smart thing to do would be to ask him... but for some reason, I'm feeling a bit uncomfortable with all the decisions.

"You okay, beauty?"

I blink up at him, shaken from my thoughts. "Yeah... just a lot to choose from."

He nods, looking down at his own menu. "Anything in particular sound good?"

I shrug, feeling silly for being so indecisive.

He gives me a knowing look. "You can get anything you want, babygirl."

I chew my bottom lip. "The chicken tenders sound good... but so does the macaroni and cheese..."

Colt smiles. "You could always get the chicken tenders with the mac and cheese on the side."

"That sounds good," I say, returning his smile.

I'm surprised when our waitress ends up being Tessa. "Hello Tessa," Colt greets.

"Hey Colt," she says, then turns to me with a wide smile. "Hi, Darlene. How're you?"

"Good. You?"

She shrugs. "I'm great. Just filling in for Amber-Lynn. Are you going to stick around and play after dinner?"

"Yeah, I think so?" I look at Colt in question.

"We can do whatever you want, babygirl."

Tessa makes a little 'aw' sound. "Well, my shift ends in about an hour, if you're still around if you want to hang out some."

I smile wide at being invited; I didn't realize how much I miss having girlfriends until I had dinner with Melinda. Laughing and chatting with another woman is different than hanging out with a man. Don't get me wrong, I love spending any time I can with Colt, but having female friends is definitely something I need in my life. I miss Charity like crazy, and without her here, I'm essentially friendless.

"We'll be here," Colt answers for me. He then places our order getting me the chicken tenders and mac and cheese and himself the salmon. I giggle when he asks to substitute the brussels sprouts for the mac and cheese.

"Shouldn't you eat your veggies?" I tease.

"I could always get them for you, little girl."

My face screws up in a grimace. "No, thank you. I'm happy with what you picked for me."

He chuckles. "That's what I thought."

"THAT WAS SO MUCH FUN," I say, laying my head on the headrest and turning towards Colt. He's currently driving me home after a night at the club. When he invited me to the club tonight, I expected a bunch of dirty sexy times. There were those, the faint ache of my bottom is proof of that, but we spent a lot of time hanging out in the bar chatting with Tessa. Plus, I met several other littles and their daddies. Oh, and Ransom was there, but he mostly stood off to the side, grunting his responses and staring daggers at Tessa, who ignored him.

It was nice to hang out and meet new people. I finally feel like I could be at home here in the city. Charity would be proud of me for making friends and settling in, even if she is still mad at me for moving away.

"I'm glad you had fun."

"I really did. Tessa seems so nice and Johnny too."

Colt purses his lips. "They are both nice, but they are also troublemakers."

I snort. "And who says I'm not a troublemaker?"

He reaches across the console and tickles my side. "I say you should consider not being a troublemaker unless you want that sexy ass of yours punished."

I shift on my seat. "Pretty sure that happens even if I'm not causing trouble."

Colt throws his head back and laughs. "That is true... but you love it."

"I really do," I say with a contented sigh.

He parks and comes around to get my door like the gentleman he is, then walks me to my door.

"Do you want to come in?"

He gives me a salacious smile, his eyes burning with untamed lust. "More than anything, but if I come inside, I'll keep you up all night, and you have school in the morning."

My heart pounds, and my pussy clenches at the thought of being kept up all night by this man. He just pleasured and punished me less than an hour ago and already I'm hungry for more.

"The problem with that is...?"

He shakes his head, pushing me against the door and thoroughly kissing me. When he pulls away, my pulse is racing and I'm feeling achy between my legs. "The problem is that you need your sleep, and I would be a bad daddy if I was selfish."

I stand on tiptoe, wrapping my arms around his neck and pulling him in for a kiss. "Please, be selfish," I say against his lips.

He returns my kiss, pinning my back to the door again. His tongue strokes mine, and I whimper. "Daddy, I need you."

"Shh..." he murmurs, kissing down my neck. The door opens behind me, then slams shut behind us as he pins me to the other side of the door.

I gasp at the quick movement, then moan happily

when he rips my dress up and off. He presses me back to the door and crashes his lips to mine. I gasp when his fingers slip into my panties. He circles my clit with his thumb and pushes two thick fingers inside me.

"Colt!"

My head thumps against the door as his fingers work magic between my legs. I wrap my arms around him, clinging as my knees get weak from need. He deepens our kiss as the heat builds. Then he finds my g-spot with those wicked fingers of his and my climax bursts from me like a firework.

"That's it. Come all over my fingers," he growls, working my pussy until every bit of pleasure is wrung from my body.

I collapse back against the door, panting for breath. Colt pulls his fingers from my panties, then licks them clean. So hot. Even thoroughly pleasured, the sight of him licking his fingers clean of my release has me ready to drag him back to my bedroom for round two... well, round four if you count the club.

Colt catches my hands when I reach for his belt. "No, that was just for you, beauty. You need to get some sleep tonight, and if you touch me, I will lose control."

I pout at being denied. He leans in and kisses my bottom lip. "No pouting."

My lip pushes out further, and he nips it between his teeth. I groan and rub myself against the front of him. With reluctance, he pulls away. Even when I ask him to stay, he sticks to his guns and leaves me with a kiss and a 'sleep sweet.'

CHAPTER TWELVE

Colt

THE LAST TWO weeks have been the best of my life. Being with Darlene is everything I've ever wanted. She's perfect for me. Not only is our chemistry off the charts, but we have a lot of things in common. Every day I fall just a little more for her. I never thought I could be so happy. I just wish that she would trust me when I say that the school staff won't care that we are together.

I'll admit it is hot sneaking around. Stealing kisses in between classes and in the teachers' lounge. We both definitely get a little thrill out of almost being caught. Even so, I want to claim her publicly too. I want people to know that Darlene is mine. Especially since Levi fucking Troy keeps sniffing around her.

Slimy bastard.

She's not complained about it, but I know he bothers her. I've heard from Coop, even Jasper—the school police officer and fellow daddy dom—has noticed when he's been here at the school how he looks at her with some kind of possession. Being public would give me the ability to tell him to fuck off, but as it is, my hands are tied. I hate it. But I'm doing my best to respect Darlene's request—for now. If he steps one toe out of line, I won't be able to stand by.

The bell rings for the end of the school day, and excitement courses through me. I wait until the school has emptied of students, and all that's left are the few teachers that stay behind working late... my Darlene being one of those diligent teachers.

I'm practically whistling as I head to her classroom. When I get there, I admire the shapeliness of her ass as she bends over her desk, arranging papers. I quietly close the classroom door and sneak up behind her. I wrap my arms around her from behind and she lets out a little squeal.

She turns in my arms, slapping my arm. "You scared me!" she accuses.

I give her a playful swat on her bottom. "I'd apologize, but I've got a beautiful woman in my arms and I can't be sorry for it."

She melts against me with a contented sigh. "How did I get so lucky?"

I scoff, "I'm the lucky one."

She giggles. "Maybe we are both the lucky ones, daddy."

I let out a little growl and attack her lips with mine. She wraps herself around my body, kissing me back with all the pent-up passion from the day apart. It's always like this. We see each other in the halls and at lunch and have to stay at arm's length, pretending to be nothing more than coworkers, so when we see each other at the end of the day, we crash together.

My cock is instantly hard at the feel of her soft body against mine. I lift her on the desk, pushing her flowy skirt up her thighs until she can wrap her sexy legs around me. I can feel the heat from her pussy through my slacks as she rubs against my thick length. She claws at my shoulders as she kisses me fiercely.

I fist her hair, pulling her lips free of mine and tilting her head back. She lets out a moan as I lick and suck down her neck to her exposed clavicle. Her hips rock against me, rubbing her wet cunt on me. I know she's soaked. So wet that she's probably leaving a wet spot behind on my pants and I can't find it in myself to give a fuck.

I'll proudly walk out of here with a wet spot over my swollen cock if it means my girl is pleasured. I nip at her neck, and she moans low in her throat, rubbing enthusiastically against me. She completely loses herself, forgetting where we are and the risks of us getting caught. I love how wanton she gets around me. It's a heady thing knowing I can make such a prim, buttoned-up woman lose herself to her submissive side.

"Daddy," she gasps as I grip her ass and pull her harder against my cock. It begs to be let free. I want nothing more than to free my cock and plunge deep into her exquisite heat, but not here.

"Fuck, babygirl. I want inside this hot little pussy."

"Yesss..." she hisses, rocking her hips. "I want you, daddy."

I groan, pulling away, knowing that we can't take this any farther here at school. "Let's go," I say, pulling her off the desk and righting her clothes.

She looks up at me, flushed and horny. "Where?"

"I'm taking you home and I'm going to fuck you and spank your ass for being such a fucking tease."

Darlene whimpers. "Oh yes," she licks her lips, "let's do that."

"Meet me in the parking lot in five."

"But..."

"No buts, I want you and the fastest way to get what I want is for me to drive you home."

I grip the back of her neck and pull her in for one last scorching kiss, barely able to control myself enough to pull away. "Five minutes."

She holds her fingertips to her lips and nods. "Five minutes."

CHAPTER THIRTEEN

Darlene

AFTER A NIGHT OF PASSION, it's hard to get back to reality. In my apartment, Colt and I are free to be us. As soon as we leave, we go back to being Miss Larson and Mr. James. Teacher and principal. Colt is getting tired of the sneaking around, I know it. He wants to be able to show the world our budding relationship.

I can't blame him. Half of me wants to shout from the rooftops that I'm falling in love with Colton James. The other half wants to keep our relationship under wraps to prevent the judgment I know will follow. I've seen how people react to teachers who date principals and superintendents. The respect from fellow teachers goes straight out the window, thinking that the teacher is getting special treatment. I don't know how it is personally, but I've seen enough to know that I don't want that to happen to me.

"You're just being stubborn, Darlene," he argues. "It's pouring. I would give any of my co-workers a ride in this kind of weather."

I roll my eyes. "I'm not made of sugar. I won't melt. Besides," I lift up my oversized umbrella, "I have an umbrella that is great for keeping things dry."

He huffs out a frustrated breath. "I still don't like it. I should be able to drop my girlfriend off at her job."

I wrap my arms around his waist. "I love that you want to do that for me, but…"

"But you still don't want people to know about us."

With my chin rested against his chest, I look up at him with a sad smile. Despite what he thinks, this isn't easy for me either. I'm slightly resentful that we work together and have the complications of that to work around, but I can't get over the idea of keeping us secret.

"I'm sorry, daddy."

He sighs, wrapping his arms around me and dropping a kiss to my forehead. "It's okay, babygirl. I just hate that I can't fully take care of you like I should be."

"You take good care of me. The best."

Colt shakes his head but smiles down at me. "I'm glad you think so, beauty. I would do anything for you. I hope you know that."

"I know you do. You prove that every day."

Finally, after a lot of convincing, Colt agrees to let me walk to work despite the rain. Today's conversation gives me the feeling that he's not going to stick to our ruse for long, and I'm nervous about what might happen when the other faculty at Thurston find out about us.

The school is still quiet. It's the calm before the storm. The calm before the students show up and chaos ensues. It's a chaos that I love, but there is something about being in these halls while they are empty that brings a level of peace that I can't quite explain. I make my way to the teachers' lounge, saying hi to several teachers along the way.

I love how friendly and welcoming everyone has been. Despite this being a huge school with hundreds upon hundreds of students and a huge faculty, everyone has made me feel like part of the Thurston family.

The lounge is empty, and I take full advantage of the coffeemaker. I'm startled by a loud whistle behind me. I turn to see Mr. Troy—the creeper—standing in the doorway. "You look fantastic today, Darlene."

I paste on a fake smile, trying to keep the peace when all I really want to do is tell him off for being a sexist jerk. I turn back to the fridge to finish putting away my lunch.

"Want to go to lunch today? I know a great little Mexican place not far from here," he asks. I can almost feel his eyes on me, and I just know he's staring at my ass.

I show him my lunch bag as I put it in the fridge. "Thanks, but I'm covered."

He licks his lips salaciously, his gaze directly on my breasts. "Next time."

Thankfully, he turns to leave and I'm once again alone in the room. I collapse against the counter, feeling dirty and slightly worried that he's not backing down. Melinda was right about needing to stay far away from him. I'll make it my sole mission in life to keep him at a distance.

A small voice in the back of my mind tells me that if I would stop being so stubborn and bring my relationship with Colt out in the open, Mr. Troy would leave me alone. I squash down that voice with all the stronger, louder doubts I have.

I wait for a few minutes, hoping Mr. Troy has had time to get back to his classroom before I head to my own. The door swings open, and I nearly run smack dab into Melinda. "Oh! I'm sorry!"

"No worries," Melinda laughs. "Was that Mr. Troy I saw coming out of here?" she asks with her lip curled up in disgust.

"Yeah, he's insufferable."

"Is he still asking you out?" She gives me a pitying look.

"Ugh. Yes, the man couldn't catch a hint if it whacked him in the face... or elsewhere..."

Melinda giggles. "Elsewhere would maybe get the point across."

"If only..."

"Right? Enough about that..." I say, feeling the need to change the subject. Just talking about Levi Troy gives me the heebie-jeebies. "So what're you reading?" I ask, pointing at the book in her hand.

She blushes. "Oh, just a silly romance."

"I love romance books. Though I have to admit I don't read often anymore."

She looks at me like I'm crazy. Melinda is an avid reader. She's always got a book with her, and I don't think I've seen her with the same book twice.

"Don't read? I don't think I understand those words put together like that," she says with shock.

It's my turn to blush because one of the main reasons I haven't read in a while is because I've spent my nights wrapped up around the hunky principal. "I spend a lot of time in my studio."

She nods, "I can understand that. It can be hard to ignore the call of your art. I feel that with my music." The bell rings, and Melinda jumps. "I've gotta run!"

"Okay, me too. We should do lunch soon."

"Sounds good."

THE SCHOOL DAY passes in a flash, and now I'm standing in front of my closet dressed only in my robe, trying to get ready for my date with the super sexy principal.

Colt will be here to get me any minute, and I'm still trying to figure out what to wear. I have no idea where we are going. I pull out my little black dress considering it again. I lay it on the bed beside my lavender dress that borders on looking like one of my club dresses. I also pull out one of the two pairs of jeans I own that I very rarely wear, preferring my skirts and dresses.

The knock at my door has me jumping to attention. I tighten my robe and chew my bottom lip. I answer the door and am instantly glad that I didn't pick my outfit since, once again, Colt is wearing a pair of dark jeans and a button-down shirt with the sleeves rolled up to his elbows. My pussy clenches at the sight of him standing there looking stern and sexy.

"I'm sorry," I say instantly, feeling guilty for not being ready to go. "I couldn't decide what to wear." I lock my fingers together in front of me and look at my bare toes.

He strides right into my apartment and wraps me up in his arms, kissing me. All of my nerves leave me, and

I'm lost in a wave of desire. I realize that no matter what outfit I pick, he will love it because he isn't here for my clothes. For some reason, this sexy as sin man finds me utterly attractive and doesn't care what I'm wearing.

"How about I help?" he asks after he pulls away from my lips.

I nod breathlessly and lead him back to my bedroom, where the three outfits are displayed on my bed. I stand to the side, chewing my bottom lip. He approaches me and uses his thumb to pull my lip from my teeth. "Only I get to bite this sexy little lip of yours," he says, leaning in and kissing the abused flesh.

"Okay, daddy," I breathe.

"Now, let's find something for you to wear."

He looks at each outfit, giving it serious consideration. He looks at me after examining each option. He quickly discards the jeans as an option. "The purple," he declares after a minute.

I give him a sideways look, curious as to why he chose that one. "Why the purple and not the sexy little black dress?"

He picks up the dress and walks towards me. "Drop the robe, babygirl."

I instantly do what he says, dropping the robe and standing in front of him in nothing but white lace. "That's why," he says with a smile.

"I-"

"Because tonight, you're my babygirl, and the fact that you picked this dress as an option shows that is where your mindset is right now," he says, interrupting me.

He helps me put on the pretty purple dress, then

kisses the tip of my nose. "If you didn't want me to be in full-on daddy mode tonight, you would've put on that sexy black dress and not thought twice about it."

I consider his words and realize he's right. I do want him to be my daddy tonight. I want him to take control. I want to relax and be little me without a worry in the world. I want that freedom more than anything. I smile a broad smile and jump into his arms, letting myself enjoy the freedom of spontaneity. He laughs and catches me.

"Thank you, daddy."

He holds me close to him and lightly rubs my back, then squeezes my bottom, causing me to moan at the tease. He could turn that into phenomenal sex or a naughty spanking, then phenomenal sex. But he doesn't; he just holds me to him, letting me enjoy the moment.

"Anything for you, beauty. I'll always give you what you need."

After I slip on my ballet flats, I'm ready to go. Colt leads me out to his car and helps me inside. He buckles me up and kisses my cheek before walking around to the driver's side. The restaurant he takes me to is nice. A lot nicer than I usually would pick. One of those places where I never know what to order. After we are seated—Colt opts to sit beside me in the booth instead of across from me like is normal—I look at the menu, and for the second time of the night, I feel overwhelmed.

Colt pulls the menu from my hands and sets it in front of him. He leans in close and whispers in my ear. "Little girls don't have to pick what they eat. Daddy does that."

Instantly my shoulders relax, and I feel light once

more. It seems all the stress from my first days at a new school, and the worry about people finding out about Colt and I have really added up. Usually, the only thing that can relax me is a trip to a club and letting my little side run free. Now, my daddy is doing that for me in a way that I've never experienced before. It's subtle. No one else here would ever suspect anything but two people enjoying a nice meal together, but we know the truth.

Colt is my daddy, and I'm his babygirl.

I'm finishing up my dessert—caramel apple cake with vanilla bean ice cream—when I see Leon and his parents. My back straightens and my stomach falls to my toes. Colt is instantly alert to the change in me and asks what's wrong.

"Leon Zimmerman is here with his family," I whisper under my breath.

He looks up and sees them but doesn't stiffen or show any outward signs of discomfort. Of course, he doesn't care what people think of him. In his position, he doesn't need to worry. Things are different for me. I'm not only new to the school, but I'm a woman. Sexist or not, women who date in the workplace—especially dating someone who is viewed as an authority figure—is looked down upon.

Thankfully, they don't seem to notice us, or if they do, they don't say anything. Colt quickly pays the check, and we leave. My happy, carefree mood has been squashed down by the reality of our relationship. The car ride back to my place is a quiet one. I can't help thinking about people judging me and why it matters so much to me.

I don't know anyone here. Yes, I want to start off on the right foot, but does that mean I have to deny myself the potential of the best relationship I've ever had? I inwardly sigh as I fret. Vacillating between one extreme and the other. I don't even realize that we're in front of my door until Colt is taking my keys from my purse for me. I blink myself back to reality, but my troubled thoughts follow me.

"Thanks for dinner," I say by rote, knowing it's what I should say even if it's not what I want to say.

He leans in and presses his lips to mine. For the first time, that spark isn't there. I feel detached from the fire that burns bright between us. My body feels it, but my mind doesn't connect the pieces. Tears spring to my eyes. I'm fucking this up so bad. I'm so worried about if we were seen that I'm pulling away.

Colt grabs a fistful of my hair with a growl and starts backing me into my apartment. A switch flips inside me. All of my worries and concerns quiet and all that is left is this burning desire that we share. Just a simple pull of my hair has me back to the reality that Colt is mine and I am his.

"It's okay, beauty," he says lowly. "They didn't see us. Even if they did, we aren't doing anything wrong."

I open my mouth to protest, the reminder of our situation diminishing the quiet of my mind when I'm submitting to my daddy. Colt grips my hair even tighter and I relax into his hold. He leans in close and brushes his lips over my own. The softness of his kiss is in complete opposition to the firm grip on my hair.

"Relax, babygirl," he commands. And I do. I sink into the sensations he's evoking. I offer up my submission willingly. Giving him the only thing I have to give—me. "Everything is okay," he murmurs against my lips before trailing them down my neck.

"What if-"

"Hush. We'll deal with what-ifs when they happen. Not a second before."

He kisses me again, chasing the last bit of my worries away. He's right. Worrying about what-ifs isn't productive. And why worry about what *could* happen when what *is* happening at this moment is perfect?

Colt works my skirt up as he kisses and nips at my neck. He grabs ahold of my ass, hard. Reminding me who's in charge right now. As if I could forget. I moan as he squeezes and caresses my bottom. His lips work their magic along my neck and shoulder, lightly sucking—not enough to leave marks, but enough to make my toes curl.

I rub against his hardness feeling how much he desires me, and every one of my worries turns to ash in the face of this strong man in front of me. My daddy. He's everything I've ever wanted, and I refuse to screw this up.

"Naughty girl," he growls, slapping my ass.

"Daddy!" I gasp, begging for more with that one word.

Colt backs me to the couch, spinning me out until I'm laying over the arm, my ass in the air. He grips my panties tight in his fist and rips them straight off my body. The sound of rendering fabric causes my knees to shake; it's so hot. His big hand crashes down without warning, and I squeal at the sudden pain.

"Ow!" I cry out, moving my hands back to cover my exposed backside.

Colt tsks, grabbing my hands and pinning them to my lower back. "You know better, beauty. Take your punishment like the good girl you are."

"Sorry, daddy."

He rubs my ass lovingly and my body relaxes over the arm of the sofa. He spanks me again, and I let the pain sink in. I don't fight. I don't beg. I just let each slap of his palm on my exposed bottom sink deep inside my soul. He's breaking me apart and piecing me back together again with each firm smack.

He lands two more hard swats on my sit spots and I whimper, but that whimper is cut off by a moan when his fingers swipe through my wetness. A wetness that's only grown with every slap of his hand. Each one drawing my arousal out until it's covering my thighs.

His fingers press inside me, gathering that slickness, then swirling around my sensitive clit. A jolt of pleasure rushes through me, and I nearly come from just that one touch. Before I can reach my climax, his fingers move away. I whimper when his hand leaves me altogether.

"Daddy..."

He chuckles darkly, then I hear him kneeling behind me. My knees buckle and my entire body is held only by the arm of the couch when he puts his mouth where his fingers just were.

"Oh, God..."

He licks at me like I'm the most delicious thing he's ever tasted. He buries his tongue inside me, fucking me with it before running teasing circles around my clit. Pleasure sings through my veins. My whole body in tune to what Colt is doing to me. He sucks my clit, sliding a finger deep inside me. He fingers my pussy to the same rhythm as he's licking and sucking my clit. I'm on the very cusp of coming when he pulls his fingers from inside me.

"Daddy, please," I whine. "I was so close."

He slaps my thigh in reprimand. "I own your pleasure, little girl."

I moan at the tinge of pain that only ramps up my need to come. His mouth is back on me and that finger of his is drawing lazy circles around my entrance, teasing me. He dips it inside again, then trails it up to my bottom hole. I groan and clench as he teases my back entrance.

No one has ever taken me there before. The touch is both forbidden and sexy as hell. He slowly pushes his finger inside me, and it's all I can take. My nerve endings tingle and the burning stretch is nothing but white-hot pleasure. Stars dance behind my eyes as I grip the couch cushion for dear life—my orgasm rocks through me, laying waste to all others before.

"Daddy! Colt! *Ohmygod*!" I cry out. He doesn't stop moving his finger as he suckles at my clit. The pleasure goes on and on until I'm blind with it. When he finally relents, I'm floating on a high. Cloud Nine has nothing on what I'm feeling right now.

I slowly return to reality when I hear Colt's belt buckle being opened then hitting the ground. I lick my lips, wanting to give him the same pleasure he just gave me. Willing my limbs to work, I stand, then slip to my knees in front of my daddy. I lightly run my hands up his thighs, taking in his long, thick length as it bobs in front of my face.

I look up at him with desire. "My turn, daddy."

Gripping his cock in one hand and his balls in the other, I lean forward licking the pearly white drop from the tip of his cock. The salty flavor bursts across my tongue and I moan. Colt threads his fingers in my hair and pulls me further onto him.

"That's it, babygirl, suck daddy's cock."

My answer is a moan as I take him deeper. Even with his hand in my hair, he lets me set the pace. I suck hard and fast, taking more and more of him on each pass until I'm swallowing down every inch of him.

I pull off of him, gasping for breath, then do it again. His eyes burn into me, watching as I fight my gag reflex to pleasure him. Then he snaps. His fist tightens in my hair, holding me in place as he fucks my mouth.

"Naughty tease," he growls. "Making daddy lose control like this. Fuck, your mouth is perfect."

I lave the bottom of his cock as best I can as he shuttles it between my lips, wanting to make this as good as I can for him. More and more of his precome coats my tongue and I swallow, wanting more.

"Do that again," he commands roughly. "Swallow."

He pushes to the back of my throat again and I swallow, and again. He sets a slow, firm rhythm that has me swallowing around the head of him on every stroke.

"Fuck, baby, I'm coming. Swallow me down. Drink it all."

I mumble my 'yes, daddy' around his cock just before he explodes. His come floods my mouth and I struggle to keep up. I don't want to disappoint him by losing a single drop. I swallow him all down, licking his still-hard cock clean.

His hand turns gentle. He's now stroking my hair

instead of pulling as I rest my head against his thigh, trying to catch my breath.

"Thank you, babygirl. That was amazing."

I look up at him and smile proudly. He lifts me from the ground and carries me to the bedroom. He helps me take my dress off and leads me to the bathroom to brush my teeth and get ready for bed. Once I've taken care of all of that, Colt tucks me into bed.

"Aren't you going to stay?" I ask with a pout.

He presses a hard kiss to my lips. "Not tonight, love."

"Why?" My mind spirals into all kinds of negative reasons as to why he wouldn't want to stay. Before my thoughts can spiral out of control, he kisses me again.

"Stop that," he scolds, somehow knowing that I'm starting to worry about silly things again. "I have an early meeting with the school board, and I don't have a change of clothes. I would love nothing more than to crawl into that bed with you."

"Oh... I guess that's okay then."

He smirks at me. "Oh, do you?"

"Yep."

Colt leans down and kisses me again. "Sleep sweet, beauty. I'll see you in the morning."

From a distance and only as co-workers, I think morosely to myself, hating my own rule but not brave enough to change it. Shortly after he leaves, I fall into a fitful sleep.

CHAPTER FOURTEEN

Colt

IT'S BEEN over a week since Leon and his family saw us at the restaurant and nothing has come of it. Thank God. I'll admit that sneaking around the school stealing kisses is hot as hell, but I don't want Darlene to use it as an excuse to run from what is growing between us. The bell rings, shaking me out of my musings. A look at the clock tells me it's Darlene's free period. The temptation to see her is too great to ignore.

I tell Judy I'm going for a little walk around the halls and I'll be back—something I'm doing more and more frequently. I'm fairly sure she's suspicious as to my newfound love for strolling around the halls of Thurston Academy. I'm almost to Darlene's classroom when I hear the sound of her voice. A smile spreads across my face until I hear the words she's saying.

"This is inappropriate, Mr. Zimmerman..."

"That's okay, baby... we won't tell anyone," a male voice responds.

"No..."

"You can spread those pretty thighs for the principal but not me?"

There's a slapping sound and a low growl, and I'm running the rest of the way down the hall and skidding into her classroom. The scene in front of me has my blood fucking boiling. Leon fucking Zimmerman has Darlene backed against the wall. Darlene has her hands up, one covering her mouth the other one out as if expecting a blow.

"Bitch, you're going to regret that," he growls, reaching for her.

I'm on him in a second. I have him yanked away and on the ground with my knee in his back within a heartbeat.

"Oh my God, Colt!" she cries out, looking at me with tearful eyes. "Don't hurt him!"

"Don't. Hurt. Him," I snarl. "Do you know what could have happened?"

I kneel into Leon's back a little harder, making him gasp. Good. The fucker deserves a hell of a lot more than being subdued. If he weren't a student... I shake my head at the thought of what I would be willing to do in the name of Darlene. The amount of rage I have coursing through my veins tells me plenty.

"She assaulted me!" he shouts from below me.

The knee in his back is definitely not enough punishment. The asshole deserves a beat down. I pull out my phone and dial Coop. "Need you in the art room, bring the on-duty school officer," I bark into the phone as soon as he answers. I hang up before he can respond.

I look over to where Darlene is still standing against the wall. Her arms are wrapped around her torso, tears are falling down her cheeks in a torrent as she shakes. "S-sorry. This is all my fault."

"This is not your fault."

What the fuck is she getting at? Her fault. Not even close. My mind goes back to what could have happened if I hadn't been so obsessed with her that I couldn't resist coming to her classroom. Leon is a starting linebacker on the school's football team. He's easily half a foot taller than her and has at least seventy-five pounds of muscle on her. He could easily overpower her... he was going to...

"She hit me!" Leon yells, trying to buck me off of him.

I laugh darkly at that. He may be bigger and badder than my Darlene, but I'm bigger and madder than him. No, not mad. I'm livid. Murderous even. Fucking shithead touched my babygirl. Darlene is mine. I let out a low, feral growl, digging my knee even harder into his back, just barely holding back my need to pummel him.

Coop and Jasper, the school police officer, show up just before I can lose my head and beat him half to death.

"What the fuck is going on here?" Coop asks, looking between where I have Leon pinned to the floor and where Darlene is crying against the wall.

"Leon attacked Dar-Miss Larson," I correct myself, trying to preserve the promise I made her, though right now I could give a fuck about keeping our relationship secret.

"Bullshit!" Leon yells. "She hit me!"

Jasper looks at Darlene. "Is that true?"

She whimpers and nods. I'm instantly up off of Leon,

letting Coop handle him. It takes me a scant second to cross the gap between Darlene and me. Unable to help myself, I cup her cheek and look into her eyes, willing her to hear my next words. "You didn't do anything wrong. You defended yourself."

"I hit a student," she cries. "He was... I just..."

She can't make a coherent sentence through her tears. She's shaking so hard that her teeth chatter. She's pale and looks about ready to collapse. I wrap my arms around her and hold her to me. I explain what I walked in on to Jasper and he calls in for backup. Darlene pushes out of my arms, she seems to be all cried out, but she's definitely not okay.

Jasper asks her a few questions and she can barely answer. She's standing there staring where Leon was on the ground just minutes before, holding her hand like it's a live snake about to strike.

"Do you want to press charges?" Jasper asks her for the second time.

She looks at him like she's in a daze and unable to comprehend what's happening around her. She's in shock.

"Can she give her statement later? Decide what she wants to do?" I ask.

"Yeah... you should get her home." Jasper gives me a meaningful look. He knows. Of course, he does. He works at The Playground as security. He probably saw my little display of ownership the other night.

I nod as he hands her his card. "Darlene," he says, making sure she's looking at him as he talks. "You're okay now, sweetheart. Colt's going to take you home, and you'll call me when you're better. Okay?"

I'm immediately appreciative that he's using his calming daddy tones, not his cop voice. She instantly responds that she will. And lays her head against my shoulder. She shivers and I pull her closer.

"It's okay, babygirl," I croon, whispering just for her ears. "Daddy's got you."

"I want to press charges," Leon yells as he's escorted from the room in cuffs. "She hit me!"

Leon is dragged from the building, screaming the whole way. I give them a minute to get him outside before I collect Darlene's things and walk her towards the office. People are standing in doorways, teachers and students alike, trying to figure out what's happening. I shield Darlene from their prying eyes as best I can, but I know holding her like this is going to raise questions.

It's something we can deal with later. For today, I'm taking care of my girl to hell with any consequences. She can be mad at me later, but right now, she needs me, and I'll be damned if I let her stubborn insistence of keeping us private hold me back.

"Oh no!" Judy cries out when she sees the state Darlene is in as I guide her to my office. I lead her to one of the chairs and help her sit. Her lack of protest or response in general scares me, but I know she'll be fine once I get her home. "What happened?"

I briefly fill her in and tell her to find a substitute for Darlene's classes for the rest of the week. She's quick to agree, and I know she'll take care of everything. I grab my things and kneel in front of Darlene. I take her ice-cold hands in mine. "Darlene, baby, I'm going to take you home now, okay?"

She nods. "Okay, daddy," she whispers, the sound quiet as a baby mouse.

I press a fierce kiss to her forehead, again, not caring if anyone sees me taking care of her. The ride to her apartment is a quick one. I help her out of the car and lift her into my arms. I carry her to her apartment and straight to her bathroom. I slowly start to remove her clothes, careful to make sure she doesn't have any sort of negative reaction. Aside from the robotic way she helps, there is none.

I turn on the taps to hot and lead her into the shower. She shivers as the hot water rolls over her cold body. The temperature shock jerks her out of her stupor. "Oh God," she says, then bursts into tears.

I climb into the shower with her, clothes and all, pulling her into my arms, holding her tight. "It's okay," I assure, "Let it out, babygirl. I've got you."

"He-he was going to…"

I growl lowly, dangerously. "No. I won't let anyone hurt you."

"If you hadn't…"

I squeeze her in my arms harder than I should but unable to help myself. "But I did. Don't even think of what could have happened. It didn't."

"The things he said…" she sniffles. "Oh God, Colt, he knows about us."

"He saw us at the restaurant…"

"No," she says empathetically, "He knows about us… that I'm a babygirl and you're my daddy… he knows. How does he know?"

I shake my head, unsure of how he could possibly know something like that. The Playground vets its members, and everyone is extremely discreet. "I'm not sure, but I will find out," I promise. And I will. No one fucks with mine without answering for it.

Once Darlene stops shaking, I pull her from the hot shower and dry her off, wrapping her in a fluffy white towel. I lift her from her feet, unable to resist having her in my arms. I don't know that I'll ever be able to let her out of my sight again after this. She's much too precious to me to risk like that.

"I can walk," she unconvincingly protests.

"And I can carry you," I reply, kissing the top of her head. "Let me take care of you."

Darlene sinks into my embrace, dropping her token protest.

CHAPTER FIFTEEN
Darlene

I WAKE up from a fitful sleep alone in bed. I can hear Colt talking in the other room and another male voice rumbling in response. A shiver runs down my spine when I remember the events of yesterday. Not able to lay in bed another second, I get up. I wash my face, brush my teeth, and then dress in my comfiest, most ragged pajamas, not caring who is here. I need the comfort of the familiar today.

With a deep, steadying breath, I quietly pad to the living room where Colt is talking to someone. When I enter the room, their conversation halts, and Colt strides across the room to me. He wraps me up in his arms, and I breathe him in. His masculine scent soothing and familiar. He pulls away but threads his fingers through mine as he leads me further into the room.

"Darlene, this is Jasper Raines. You met him yesterday."

I nod, vaguely remembering the friendly officer that arrested Leon. "Hello, Darlene."

"Nice to see you again, Officer Raines."

"Jasper, please."

"Jasper..."

Colt gives my fingers a reassuring squeeze. "Jasper came by to talk about what happened yesterday with Leon."

Fingers of fear shiver up my spine. My grip tightens on Colt's hand. He leads me over to the couch and sits, pulling me into his lap so he can hold me close. I stiffen in his lap, unsure about showing such a blatant confession of our relationship in front of a virtual stranger. After what happened yesterday, I'm even more aware of how it'll look to other people if they know about us.

Especially if they find out the nature of our relationship, I've never been ashamed of being a little before... but yesterday has rocked my confidence. I can feel myself systematically pulling away from both Colt and that part of myself.

"It's okay, babygirl," Colt whispers in my ear. "Jasper is a member of The Playground..."

Understanding dawns, and I realize with a start that I've seen him there. He was dressed as security like Ransom.

"That's right, sweetheart. You don't have to be afraid of me," Jasper says, coming to sit on the chair across from us. "I'm a daddy dom like Colt. You're safe with me. I want to help get to the bottom of this and make sure that Leon is brought to justice."

I shiver at his name, unsure of how I'll ever return to work if just hearing his name is enough to frighten me.

What if he ruined the classroom I love? What if I can't be there without feeling this fear?

Colt's arms tighten around me, and my brain calms slightly, knowing he's here. He runs his fingers through my hair, soothing my frayed nerves. "I thought you might be more comfortable talking to Jasper here at home instead of down at the station..." Colt trails off.

I know exactly what he isn't saying. And he's right. I am more comfortable talking with Jasper knowing he's a daddy dom too. Knowing that the man who will be hearing about one of the worst things to ever happen to me won't judge my lifestyle. He'll understand things unlike anyone who isn't in the lifestyle.

"You're right," I say to Colt before turning to Jasper and asking him what he needs to know.

"Just start from the beginning and tell me what happened. Take your time, sweetheart. There's no rush. You're safe here." Jasper speaks in soothing tones like he would to a frightened animal. I suppose I could be seen as the same since I'm tensed and ready to jump at the slightest provocation. I'm still in fight or flight mode, and right now, flight is the only thing on my mind.

"He stayed after class..." I start my side of things, then worry floods me. What did Leon tell them? I can vaguely remember him shouting about me assaulting him. Screaming that I should be arrested.

"I hit him," I say, suddenly cutting myself off. "Are you going to have to arrest me? I hit a student—a minor. I'm going to lose my job..." My breathing turns erratic at the implications of what I did. The thoughts pile up until I'm struggling to catch my next breath.

Colt croons quietly to me that I'm okay and to just

breathe, but how can I be okay? He doesn't know. Jasper could be here right now to take my statement before locking me in cuffs and dragging me down to the station.

As if he knows that nothing Colt says will calm my spiral, Jasper gets on his knees in front of me and grips both of my hands between his strong ones. "Breathe, sweetheart," he calmly says. "You're not going to jail. First of all, he isn't a minor. Secondly, you won't be losing your job."

I stare at him wide-eyed. "Are you sure?"

Colt holds me a little tighter. "He's right, Darlene, you didn't do anything wrong. It was self-defense, and anyone who thinks otherwise will be put in their place quickly."

My building anxiety shrinks down to a manageable level again. It's definitely not gone, but it's calmed enough that I can finish giving Jasper my statement.

I tell them how he claimed to need help on his project, but as soon as we were alone, it was like a switch had flipped. His All-American boy next door mask that he wears disappeared completely and was replaced with a look of disgust. I tell them about how he backed me into the wall and caged me in with his arms so I couldn't get away. How he threatened to tell everyone about my sick relationship with Colt if I didn't sleep with him.

Leon went into great detail about all the things he wanted to do to me... those things were the hardest to open up about, and even with Jasper and Colt's praise at my bravery, I really wanted just to skip all of that. I push through, telling them the worst of it, and by the time I'm done with my side of things, I'm utterly exhausted.

Jasper asks a few more questions, then leaves with

the assurance that everything is going to be okay and that I don't have to worry about Leon anymore. Colt walks him out, talking in low tones. Part of me wonders what they are talking about. The other part can't be bothered to find out.

"Are you hungry, babygirl?" Colt asks once he shuts and locks the door.

My body must still be in shock since I don't feel any hunger pangs even though I haven't eaten since breakfast yesterday. I shake my head, "Not really."

He frowns at me. "You need to eat something. How about I make you some soup and a grilled cheese?"

I think about it for a second and then nod. "Okay, I can try to eat."

Before going to the kitchen to make my meal, he comes over and covers me with the throw blanket from the back of the couch. He flicks on the TV and turns it to my favorite baking show, then leans in and kisses me softly.

My heart thumps in my chest, and for the first time, I doubt myself and if Colt and I can survive the fact that our coworkers now know that we are together. There's no way that rumors haven't spread like wildfire through the school after the way Colt practically carried me from the school. This is the kind of thing that gets everyone talking and speculating.

This is the exact thing I was afraid of happening. Add the extra drama surrounding Leon and his thwarted attack and it's a recipe for judgment. I'm not sure how I feel about our relationship being brought into the open. Relief? Fear?

Look how Leon responded to knowing... He knew

about our BDSM relationship. Did he tell other people? Do they know about the nature of Colt and I's relationship? Do they think we are just dating, or do they know we are kinky?

Shame and fear burn in my belly. I don't have time to dwell on my feelings because Colt comes back into the room with a steaming bowl of soup and a grilled cheese. My stomach growls at the smell proving that I am, in fact, starving.

"How are you feeling?" he asks after I finish my soup.

I shrug. "I'm okay. A little overwhelmed still. Nervous about what the school might be saying about me right now."

He nods. "I talked to Judy this morning. She put out a statement to the faculty about what happened with Leon." At the look of fear on my face, he quickly adds, "Only about his attack. There have been several people asking about our relationship, and I thought it best to be as transparent as possible." He looks at me uncomfortably, knowing that whatever he's about to say is going to go against my feelings on the subject. "I confirmed that we are dating. Everyone was speculating on our relationship, and it just seemed wiser to confirm it than to make up some elaborate lie."

I nod. Having things confirmed and out in the open is a bit of a relief now that I know for sure that people know. However, it brings up those fears of judgment I've been stressing over ever since I realized that Colt is the principal of the school.

"No one is judging you, babygirl. Everyone is just concerned about you and if you're okay after being attacked. I assure you, us being together isn't even a blip on their radar."

I let out a sigh that was practically dragged out from the tip of my toes. "I knew it was going to happen sooner or later. I just hope you're right."

He takes my empty bowl and plate to the kitchen and cleans them up. He comes back into the room, and I notice he's wearing the same clothes from yesterday. "I need to run home and get a few things. Will you be okay here alone, or would you like to come with me?"

I chew on my lip, wondering if it will hurt his feelings if I tell him he can just stay at home. Everything has happened so fast, I kind of want to lock myself in my studio and ignore the outside world for the rest of the day. I don't want to be reminded about what happened anymore, and having Colt here is a huge reminder of how my life here is about to change.

"I'll be fine. In fact, you can stay at your house. I don't need to be babysat."

He frowns at me. "Are you sure? I'd feel better staying with you, babygirl."

I know he is just concerned, but still, I bristle. "I'm fine, Colt. I just need some time alone."

He reluctantly agrees and leaves a few minutes later, promising to come check on me in the morning. Once he's gone, I immediately regret sending him away. Being alone with my thoughts definitely isn't a good thing, but it's already too late. The doubts have crept in, and pushing them out is a war I'm not strong enough to fight.

CHAPTER SIXTEEN
Colt

Despite my misgivings, I leave Darlene's apartment without putting up a big fight. Leaving is the last thing I want to do. I can feel the emotional distance she's trying to put between us, and I fear that this physical distance will only add to it. The last thing I want to do is suffocate her, though, so I'll give her what she wants.

Instead of going home, I head to Thurston and the gym to work off some of the pent-up rage from what could have happened to Darlene. I spend hours running and lifting until my muscles burn and my mind is quiet save for the worry I have for my girl.

I sleep like absolute shit. Missing the warm weight of my babygirl in my arms. Wishing that we were together. Wondering if she's okay or not. I'd be lying if I said that I didn't wake up early just so I could hurry over to see Darlene. When she opens her door, I feel like I take a breath for the first time since I left.

Darlene looks like she hasn't slept at all. The second I lay eyes on her, I pull her into my arms. She's stiff for a second but then sinks into my hold. She hugs me back for long minutes, and all is right in the world again.

"I missed you, beauty."

"I missed you, too, but you didn't have to come by this morning. I know you need to get to school."

I scoff. "You're more important. Besides, I planned to stay here with you today."

She frowns. "You should go to work like it's a normal day."

"What? Why would I do that when you need me?" I ask, taken aback.

"Because if you're at school, you can stop any rumors from spreading... maybe find out exactly what people know. If anyone else knows about the BDSM aspect of our relationship..." She whispers that last part and almost looks ashamed.

With a knuckle under her chin, I lift her face to mine. "You have nothing to feel ashamed for... we are both consenting adults. So what if you're a babygirl? So what if I'm a daddy dom? There are way more of us out there than you'd think. Heck, there are several working at the school."

She closes her eyes in a grimace. "I just don't like the thought of people judging me. You know how people can be. I don't want to be known as the pervert."

I wrap her up in my arms again. "You're not at fault here, Darlene. I think you're wrong about people judging us—you. I have faith that everything is going to work out."

"I hope you're right," she says morosely.

With even more reluctance than last night, I leave Darlene's apartment and a huge piece of my heart behind. If she feels better knowing that people aren't talking about her, then I'll do everything in my power to stop any incorrect rumors before they spread like wildfire.

The first thing I do is call everyone in for a staff meeting before school starts, deciding it's best to start off with complete transparency.

Melinda is one of the first teachers in the room. She shyly comes up to me with a look of concern on her face. I know she is close to Darlene, and I'm sure she's more worried than most.

"Is it true that Mr. Troy attacked Darlene?" she asks in hushed tones.

My brow furrows at the question. Is that the rumor going around? Or just an assumption on Melinda's part? "No, it was Leon Zimmerman."

She gasps. "A student attacked her?"

I nod gravely. "Yes, it seems he saw us together and decided to get revenge for missing out on two important games."

"I just assumed... I mean, all of us girls sort of thought it was Levi because he disappeared after you took Darlene home."

"He did?"

"Yeah, we all had to scramble to help cover his classes. I just... I mean, he'd been borderline harassing her since she started. I can't believe it was a student."

The wheels in my head are turning, trying to figure out why Levi would disappear like that. I know it wouldn't have been out of concern for Darlene nor Leon. Is he connected to her attack in some way? I make a note to talk to Jasper as soon as the meeting is over. If anyone can find out why he cut out without a word, it's him.

"Okay, now that we are all here, I want to discuss what occurred yesterday. I'm sure some of you have already heard Miss Larson was attacked in her classroom yesterday—" I have to pause because of all of the gasps. "I've heard there's a rumor going around that Mr. Troy was the one involved. That is incorrect. Leon Zimmerman is the one who attacked her. He was arrested, and she is pressing charges."

There are more gasps and whispers. I raise my hand to quiet everyone down. "Another thing that I want to disclose is that Darlene and I are seeing each other. I know several of you were questioning this, and I don't want rumors flying around. Yes, we are dating."

Many people smile, and there are congratulations thrown out there. No one looks scandalized or shocked even. I have to wonder if we were as discreet in our sneaking around as we thought we were being. Either way, everyone is supportive. There is an outpouring of well-wishes for Darlene, and many asking if there is anything they can do for her. She quickly became a part of the Thurston family with her sweet demeanor and helpful attitude. Everyone adores her. I promise to pass along the well-wishes and dismiss everyone to get ready for classes to start.

"Hey, Coop," I call out before he can leave too. "Can I have a word?"

He nods and follows me into my office. "What's up?"

"Did Jasper tell you the details of what happened?"

"Only the basics. Why?" he asks, concerned.

"Somehow, Leon knew the nature of our relationship. Not just that we are seeing each other. He said some... concerning things regarding it. One of the only reasons I agreed to come in today was because of how worried Darlene is about people talking about her. She doesn't want people judging her for dating me, let alone for the kind of relationship we have."

Coop's eyes grow wide, and he shakes his head. "How would that little fuck know? Someone at The Playground? No one would talk to him... or anyone for that matter. All the members sign non-disclosures."

"I just don't understand how he could've found out. Have you heard anything about Levi being out?" I ask. "Melinda told me he took off yesterday without telling anyone, and he wasn't at the staff meeting today."

"I haven't heard anything. Want me to ask Jasper to look into it?"

"Yeah, do that." If anyone can get to the bottom of what's going on with Levi, it's Jasper. Whether through legal methods... or questionable ones, he will figure out what the little fucker is up to. I don't like the timing of him disappearing from school at the same time as the attack. Something isn't adding up, and I want to know why.

I'M GOING through emails when there's a knock on my office door. Judy is at lunch, or she would've announced who is here. I've had a lot of people dropping in today asking if there is anything they can do for Darlene. It's sweet but fucking exhausting.

"Come in," I call out. The door swings open, and

Jasper strides in with a grim look on his face. "Hey, man. Did you find out anything?"

Jasper's eyes narrow as he flops down into one of the chairs across from my desk. He tosses a file folder onto my desk. Warily, I open the folder finding it full of pictures. Pictures of what looks like a fucking shrine to Darlene. Dozens of pictures wallpaper a wall. Pictures of her walking to school, teaching class, smiling with Melinda, her head thrown back in laughter at something... Pictures of us walking into The Playground, of us on our date the night that Leon and his parents saw us, even some of us here at school together. Then more disturbing are the next set of pictures... Me coming and going into her apartment with vivid red x's drawn over my face.

I look up at Jasper. "What the fuck is this?" I growl, feeling a fierce protectiveness clawing at my throat, knowing that my Darlene is home alone right now and someone is obviously stalking her.

"Levi Troy has fallen off the map. When I couldn't track him down, I called in a couple favors for a search warrant for his apartment and found this." He waves his hand toward the file I'm still thumbing through. "It seems he has a little bit more than a simple infatuation with Darlene. The fucker is obsessed. And he's none too happy that you're dating her."

"So you think Troy put Leon up to attacking Darlene?" I growl, feeling positively feral with my anger.

Jasper shrugs. "I assume so, but Leon isn't talking. His lawyer wants no part of any conversation that doesn't include him getting off without a record."

"No fucking way," I spit. "Darlene is pressing

charges. That little asshole is going to burn as far as we are concerned."

His lips twitch up in a smile. "That's almost verbatim what I told them... except you were nicer."

I laugh darkly. "As long as everyone knows where we stand on the matter. Now what the fuck are we going to do about Troy?"

"Already have a warrant out for him. I put Ransom on Darlene's apartment building."

"I thought he retired?" I ask.

"He did, but he's more than happy to pull out some of his training to protect one of our own."

"Good. I wouldn't trust anyone more than him with her safety." And it's true. Ransom is ex-military and used to run his own private security business before deciding to retire and take on a job with fewer bullets flying his way. If anyone can keep my girl safe, it's him.

"Don't worry, Colt. We'll find the bastard."

"He better pray you find him first."

Jasper chuckles. "Here's hoping. I'd hate to have to arrest you for assault."

"It would be well worth it," I growl.

"Indeed." Jasper grabs the folder from my desk and heads to the door. "We'll find him. Until then, just focus on Darlene."

THE REST of the day crawls by. When the final bell rings, I'm out the door and heading to Darlene's place. I've been itching to hold her since I left her apartment this morning, and the desire has grown to a fever pitch since seeing those pictures Jasper brought.

Darlene opens her door on the second knock. She's still in the same clothes she was wearing yesterday, and her hair is in a messy knot on top of her head. She looks nothing like her usual happy self. She'd look beautiful in a burlap sack, but she seems almost defeated, and I hate it.

She welcomes me inside with a hug. She holds onto me like she's not sure she will ever get to hold me again. Wariness prickles down my spine, tripping warning bells in my mind. I brush it off as her just being upset and in need of comfort.

"How was school?" she quietly asks. I know what she's not saying. She wants to know if rumors are going around and what they are about.

"Everything is okay. I called a staff meeting and laid everything out so that there won't be any rumors. I told the faculty about Leon—a very watered-down version of what occurred. I also explained that you and I are in a relationship."

Darlene flinches at that. I know she wants to keep us a secret, I knew this would be the hardest part, but at least I can tell her with confidence that no one in the school is judging our relationship. None of the things she's been worried about have come to pass.

"Don't worry, beauty. No one was shocked. In fact, everyone was happy for us. I was asked multiple times what people could do for you. They are all just upset that you were attacked at school. No one cares about us."

"For now. They only care about the sensationalism of

the attack. When that wears off, they will start talking about us. I know how this story goes, Colt. Eventually, someone is going to think you're playing favorites or worse. This sort of thing never ends well."

Cold chills race through me at that. Is she thinking about ending things? Why would she say it like that? "What do you mean, 'never ends well?'"

She throws her hands out and paces away from me. "I mean exactly that. Relationships like ours eventually cause drama within the faculty. Heck, the student body is impacted too. Look at Leon."

I growl. "Leon was not a normal situation."

Darlene sighs, "I know. I'm sorry... I'm just–"

I tug her back into my arms, holding her close. "It's okay, baby. I know this is hard."

She nods sniffling. I hate myself a little for what I have to tell her. My anger at Levi Troy grows even higher, knowing he's forcing me to upset my girl even further. Part of me hopes that I can get my hands on him before the police just to make him pay for every tear Darlene cries.

"I need to tell you something..."

She looks at me with wide, tearful eyes. "What is it?"

"Let's sit down..." I pull her along with me to the couch and sit with her on my lap. "There's no easy way to tell you this, but I want you to know that you're safe. Nothing is going to happen to you."

"You're scaring me, Colt."

"I'm sorry, babygirl. I don't want to scare you... Levi Troy has been stalking you," I say bluntly, ripping off the band-aid. "We aren't positive, but we think that he put Leon up to attacking you."

"What do you mean that he's been stalking me?" Her tone is wary, if not a little fearful.

"I mean, he's been following you... us. His house is full of pictures of you. He's obsessed."

"I don't understand. He's flirted some and asked me out a couple times... I've always turned him down. Why...?" She shakes her head, probably trying to wrap her mind around the information I just gave her.

"He's a sick man. There's no way to know how his mind works or why he would start stalking you."

"Is it because of us?"

"No, babygirl. Regardless if we were together or not, he would have still gotten to the same place. He's sick. It has nothing to do with you, not really. You didn't do anything to encourage his behavior."

CHAPTER SEVENTEEN
Darlene

STALKED.

The very thought is ludicrous. Who would want to stalk me? I'm a nobody. But based on the fact that I'm being trailed on my walk to school by Ransom from The Playground—apparently, he's a retired bodyguard and ex-military. Both Jasper and Colt were adamant that he play bodyguard to me until Levi is caught.

I only put up a token protest because, let's be honest, I'm freaked the heck out. When Colt told me a couple days ago about the stalking, it didn't seem real to me. Then Jasper brought a file folder full of evidence of his stalking, and the fear crept in. Especially when I saw the pictures of Colt's face crossed out in big, bold red marker. My anxiety is so high that I'm barely sleeping. Even with Colt beside me, I can't seem to sleep soundly.

It's been four days, and no one has seen or heard from Levi, and Leon still refuses to talk. Colt and I spent the weekend holed up at my apartment. We watched movies and ate delivery food. I probably gained ten pounds in pizza and Chinese food weight, but I have zero regrets. Living in our little bubble was perfect. I was able to ignore my worries about people at work knowing we are dating and mostly ignore the fact that I have a stalker.

Now reality has flooded in and overwhelmed me. It's Monday morning, my first day back to school since the attack, and I'm walking around like some kind of bait for a crazed stalker. Wait, that's precisely what I am... Bait.

It was my choice. Even though I'm scared half to death, I told Jasper I would continue on like I have no idea anything is wrong. That I would walk to school and pretend that nothing is happening beyond it being a typical Monday. Colt wasn't at all excited about the idea but relented when I was adamant that I wanted to do it.

Now I'm cursing myself because even with Ransom discreetly following me, I don't feel safe. I feel exposed like I can almost feel the lens of a camera on me. Jasper and Ransom assured both Colt and I that I'll be completely safe, that this is only to try to flush Levi out so he can be caught faster, but all of a sudden, it feels like a terrible idea. I pick up the pace, wanting desperately to get to the school and the safety that the walls will provide.

I worried that I wouldn't feel safe there after Leon's attack, but knowing that Colt is there along with Jasper and my friends, it feels like the safest place to be. I practically run up the stairs to the front door of the school. I burst into the entryway and almost collapse in sheer relief.

Colt is standing in the doorway to the office—having

agreed not to meet me at the front door in case Levi was following me. They didn't want to tip Levi off that we know that he's stalking me. I practically run into Colt's arms. It's not until he's holding me that I realize I'm shaking.

"Shh. It's okay, babygirl. You're safe," he croons.

I take a deep breath and settle my nerves. "I'm okay," I agree, taking a step back from him. "I'm okay," I say more firmly, and with every bit of confidence I can muster up. It's not much, but it's enough to take me out of wilting violet territory.

Jasper comes into the office, giving my shoulder a reassuring squeeze. "You did well."

"Did you see him?" I want the answer to be yes. I don't want to have to live in fear. It's only been a few days since I found out about Levi Troy stalking me, and I already feel like I've been scared for years. I don't think I can live this way. The desire to hole up in my apartment is huge.

"No, sweetheart. If he's watching, he's being careful. Don't worry, we'll keep you safe," Jasper says reassuringly.

I'm glad for such capable men watching over me but having them here isn't nearly as reassuring as one would think. How long can they watch over me? Days? Weeks? Months? The idea of this going on for months or even weeks has my anxiety spiking. I can't live this way. I mentally shake myself. Colt will make sure I'm safe. He won't let anything happen to me. I repeat it like a mantra. Slowly, my heart rate slows and the hand clutching my chest releases.

The bell rings, and I jump. Colt squeezes my hand

and murmurs that it's okay. I laugh a little at my jumpiness. "Sorry, I'm being ridiculous," I say to the men.

Both of them give me hard looks. "You have nothing to be sorry about," Colt says. "You're handling everything really well, considering."

I laugh a little manically. "If this is me handling things well..."

"Don't be so hard on yourself. This isn't something anyone can prepare for," Jasper says. "I don't want you to worry today. Just go about your day like you normally would."

Easy for him to say. He's not the one who has a psychopath stalking him. They've all promised I'll never be alone, that someone will always be watching over me, even when it seems they're not. I release a deep breath, deciding to trust that they can keep me safe. What else is there to do?

"Okay. Normal..."

The warning bell rings, and it's time for me to head to class. Colt gives me a quick kiss and I woodenly leave, feeling the cold fingers of dread creeping in.

I'm halfway to my room when I see Melinda. With a happy squeal, the slight woman throws herself at me and hugs me tight. "I'm so glad you're okay. I've been so worried about you," she says.

I hug her back, thankful to have found such a great friend. "I'm okay," I say even though it's only partially true. I'm fine from the attack she's talking about but more messed up over the Levi Troy stalking crisis. We—meaning the guys protecting me—decided to keep the stalking under wraps for now. I agreed because I don't want him potentially harming anyone else.

Mel and I walk side-by-side towards our classrooms. "So, Mr. James, huh?" she asks with a teasing smirk.

My cheeks flush pink, and I'm brought out of the worry for a moment and into the fact that my friend now knows about my boyfriend and he's no longer a secret. "Yeah..."

"I'm happy for you. Colt's a good man."

"Thanks. I'll admit, I'm nervous about everyone knowing. I don't want anyone to feel like I get special treatment because I'm dating him."

Mel] rolls her eyes. "Not at all. He's a fair man. Honestly, we are all happy for him. He's been alone for a long time and he deserves to be happy."

"Do you think he's happy?" I ask.

"We were all speculating on why the man was walking around the school with a smile on his face. Before you, he was a bit of a surly grump."

Colt? A grump? I've never seen him surly or grumpy. He's been my stern daddy often enough, but he's never been grumpy around me. Well, he's been downright pissed off over what happened with Leon and now Levi, but those are extenuating circumstances. I can't imagine him being anything but the smiling, warm-hearted man he's been with me since day one.

Yes, he's a stern disciplinarian, but that's also something that doesn't count. That's all part of being my daddy. It's always tinged with a softer emotion. We're at my classroom before I have time to really dissect what she's saying.

"Lunch?" Mel asks.

I want to say yes, but at the same time can't imagine leaving the safety of the school. I chew on my lip as I waffle between living my life normally like Jasper said or being a fraidy cat and eating lunch here. Fraidy cat wins. "I've got a lot to catch up on, maybe a quick one in the lounge?"

She gives me a happy smile. "Sounds good. Good luck today. I know your students have been worried."

"Thanks."

She waves over her shoulder on her way to her own classroom.

The first half of the day flies by. It turns out my students were worried about me—even Todd, who gave me a hard time that first day alongside Leon. Without Leon's influence, Todd is a good kid. I have high hopes for him now that he's seen Leon's true colors. Maybe he can make better decisions than his friend encouraged.

I'm exhausted from fielding questions from my students about what happened and if I'm okay. I didn't realize how much it would take out of me to have to tell even the bare bones of the story over and over. By the time lunch rolls around, I'm ready for a break from my beloved classroom.

Halfway to the teachers' lounge, I notice Coach Cooper following me. I turn and give him a startled glance. He gives me a warm smile and closes the distance between us. "Sorry, Darlene, I didn't mean to startle you. I'm helping Colt and Jasper keep an eye on things. I thought they told you," he says lowly as to not be overheard.

I let out a sigh of relief. Of course Colt would have

his best friend watching out for me. It only makes sense. "Of course!" I say brightly, faking some of my usual perky self. "I should've guessed the guys would rope you into this thing."

He gives me a look that is all at once stern and concerned. "I volunteered to watch over you. No one deserves to go through what you did. And this whole business with Levi Troy," he hisses. "Well, let's just say, I won't be one bit disappointed if I have to knock him down a few pegs."

I giggle a little at that. "I would love it if he got knocked down more than a few."

Coop's lips tilt up in something like a smile but looks a little feral and a lot angry. "No worries, he's going to get his comeuppance."

We chit chat about nothing in particular the rest of the way to the lounge. He tells me to stay safe and that he'll be watching—which sounds way creepier than it is. I walk into the room and everyone falls silent. Apparently, I've been the topic of conversation. I try to brush it off, but some of the judgmental looks I'm getting make it hard. This was the exact reason I wanted to keep my relationship with Colt quiet.

Too late now.

I grab a bag of chips from the vending machine, having forgotten to pack a lunch this morning with everything else going on. I sit at the only empty table and try to focus on the chips. A few minutes later, Mel comes bustling into the room, an apologetic look on her face as if she knows what I walked into, and she's sorry that she wasn't here to brave the silent glares with me. She pops her lunch into the microwave then sits with me, glaring at Karen at the other table.

I'm guessing she's the ringleader of the people who are displeased that I'm dating Colt. I try to find discomfort at the thought of her judgment, but there is none. With what is happening with Levi, I can't be worried about someone so trivial as a jealous woman who probably wanted Colt for herself.

Mine. I think with an internal growl—all mine.

Mel and I chat about school and her newest romance book that she promises to let me read when she's done. Apparently, it's written by an amazing independent romance author who can spin a story that's both intriguing and hot as hell. Plus, all of the heroes are sexy bikers, and the heroines are damaged, but with a steely will to carve out their own happiness despite everything they've been forced to survive.

I readily agree to read the book after her. Who doesn't need a growly hero in their life? Speaking of growly heroes, I can't help but wonder where my own hero is at. I thought for sure Colt would be in the lounge waiting for me, but he's nowhere to be seen. I'm tempted to text him. I keep my phone in my bag by sheer force of will, not wanting to be clingy.

I finish my chips and decide to head back to my classroom to work on grading projects. Mel walks with me, and we part ways at my classroom. I tuck my things away in my bottom drawer then notice an envelope on my desktop. I turn it over in confusion, wondering what it is. If it's from the school, it goes into our mailboxes inside the office. Maybe a student?

I open the envelope and gasp at what I see. A deep

well of sickness opens up in my stomach, and anxiety courses through my body. It's an envelope of pictures. All of them have Colt in them, all of them are destroyed in some way. The ones that are the most disturbing have burn marks on them. A note falls out of the envelope, and I pick it up with shaking hands.

I don't like obstacles. Don't make me hurt him.

I read the words over and over, knowing exactly who this is from and what it means. How did he get this in here? A cold breeze flutters my hair, and I realize one of the windows to the classroom is open. Would Levi have crawled in through a window? Shivers wrack my body, and I quickly close the window and throw the lock. I double-check all of the locks on the windows and close the blinds.

My room is now thrown into shadow without the bright light of the sun shining in. It does nothing to dispel my anxiety. I grab my phone and lock myself in the small bathroom off my classroom. I pull up Charity's phone number and dial. I know she's probably got a class, but I need to talk to her now.

"Dar?" she asks breathlessly. "What's wrong?"

I let out a sob. "S-sorry to bother you. I just... I don't know who else to call."

"It's okay," she says to me, then yells, "Pick up your feet, girls! Fast foot forward."

"Lazy assed kids. Now, take a deep breath and tell me what's wrong."

"My stalker. H-he left an envelope with pictures on my desk. A th-threat to hurt Colt. He said he doesn't like obstacles. Charity, I think he's going to hurt Colt if I don't break up with him."

Charity sighs. "Hon, calm down. Colt is a big boy. He can take care of himself."

"I couldn't live with myself if he got hurt because of me."

"Doesn't he deserve the chance to know what's happening? He could have a solution that would keep you both safe," she says, logically.

But right now, logic isn't making any sense. All I can think about are those mutilated images of Colt. I don't know what Levi Troy is capable of, but I think he might just be crazy enough to hurt Colt if I don't break up with him.

"What if he can't?" I ask quietly. "What if I just get us both hurt?"

"You're about to do something insane like break up with him, aren't you?"

"What other choice do I have?" My tears are falling in rivers down my cheeks now at just the thought of breaking things off. How will I ever break up with him? He'll know the second I do that something is up unless I come up with a good excuse. Colt isn't the kind of man to just give up on someone.

"Uh. Talking to Colt and letting him decide if he wants to take the risk or not, for starters."

"Why must you always make sense?"

She laughs. "Seriously, Darlene, just talk to Colt. Don't do anything rash."

"Thanks, Cha-cha."

"Anytime. I better get back to these girls before they think it's naptime. Call me later. Love you, girl."

"Love you too."

I dry off my tears and collect myself. Class will be

starting soon. I need to get my crap together. The rest of the day is a blur of looking over my shoulder and fending off questions about Leon from my students. To say the afternoon was a rough one is putting it mildly.

When the final bell of the day rings, I feel an immense amount of relief. I get my stuff together—shoving the envelope of pictures to the bottom of my bag—and head to the office like Colt, Jasper, and I discussed this morning. Judy waves as she leaves for the day, then I'm in the office alone with the man I'm falling in love with.

"Babygirl," Colt says with something like relief.

I close the small distance between us and sink into his arms. My eyes fall closed as I rest against his chest, feeling safe and secure for the first time since I left him this morning. I feel completely drained and exhausted. Even knowing I'm being protected hasn't eliminated my fears. Now that I know he can get to me even with people watching, I feel even more vulnerable.

"Hey, hey," Colt says, cupping my cheek and turning my head up so I'm looking at him. "What's wrong?" he asks, wiping tears from my cheek with his thumb.

I didn't even realize I was crying. I've become quite the sad sack today. It's obvious that I don't handle stress well. At least, not of the stalker variety. I almost laugh at that. Someone is stalking me? Of all the people in the world, why would he fixate on me?

"Just relieved to see you." Though that's only part of the truth. The biggest reason for my tears is that this is quite possibly the last time I'll be held by Colt like this until this whole thing is over and Levi is caught. Maybe longer if he doesn't forgive me for what I'm about to do.

"I missed you too, babygirl," he says, kissing me sweetly. I open for his stroking tongue, offering myself up to him. Our kiss is slow and savoring. He runs his fingers through my hair, tilting my head exactly how he wants it, deepening the kiss.

My heart sings at being reunited with Colt. Everything in my being wants to crawl into his lap and let him hold me until everything is right in the world. But that's not how the world works, and I have no choice but to make the hard decision to break things off.

"Are you ready?" he asks.

I shudder at the reminder that I get to walk home by myself and see if we can flush Levi out. "No... but yes. I just want this whole thing over."

"Me too. We'll catch him soon and things can go back to normal."

I give him a sad smile and a nod. He gives me a curious look but doesn't call me on my non-answer. Nothing will be normal again after I break things off with him. Like a chicken, I don't break up with him in person. No, I kiss him, pouring every bit of my desire and love into it deciding to take the easy way out and break things off by phone.

Wrapping my arms around myself, I make my way home, desperately trying not to run like I want to. I do my best to remind myself that Ransom is out there somewhere looking out for me. I'm in no danger. I repeat it to myself like a mantra until I get to my apartment. I let out a little scream when someone steps out of the shadows. Jasper.

"Sorry, sweetheart. I didn't mean to scare you. I'm

here to look through your apartment to make sure there're no surprises inside."

I nod, still holding my hand to my throat. My heart is racing a mile a minute, and I'm so on edge that I can't get my key in the lock. Jasper's big hand takes the keys from me and unlocks the door for me.

"Thanks."

He walks into the apartment, and I follow. He does a cursory look through the front room, then pulls me inside and puts me in front of the wall beside the door. He shuts and locks the door and tells me to stay put before he goes through the rest of my apartment.

"Everything is good."

"Thanks for doing this for me... I know it's not exactly your job," I say, indicating his uniform.

"My job is to serve and protect. I say this is exactly what I need to be doing right now."

"I appreciate it."

After making sure I don't need anything else, Jasper leaves, instructing me to lock and chain the door. Which I do the second it closes behind him. My phone rings in my bag, and I grab it seeing it's Colt.

"Hey, babygirl. I'm going to stop and pick us up some dinner. What sounds good?" he asks.

"I... um... well, I think maybe you shouldn't come over tonight. Maybe if I'm alone Levi will-"

I can hear Colt suck in a breath. He absolutely wants to argue with me. Though, the fact that I'm walking to and from school alone, it arguably makes sense to not have him here. Besides the fact that him not being here keeps him safe...

"If you're sure?"

No, I want to shout. "Yeah. It just makes sense."

Nothing about being without Colt makes sense, I think to myself.

"Okay... if you're sure you'll be okay."

"I'm not sure how I feel about anything, honestly. But Ransom is watching, and Jasper checked my apartment for me. It makes sense to give Levi every opportunity to make his move. Get this whole thing over with faster—I hope."

"I don't like it," Colt growls lowly, sending shivers down my spine. "I should be there to keep you safe, not serving you up like some kind of treat."

"It'll be okay, daddy," I whisper, wondering if this will be the last time I call him that. My heart breaks into a million pieces at the thought.

"Stay safe, babygirl. Call me if you need me. I'll be there in ten minutes."

"I will. Goodnight, daddy."

"Night," he says, disconnecting the call.

"I love you," I say to myself because, at this moment, I realize how true those words are. I've fallen in love with Colt. But it doesn't matter. I'll break my own heart to keep him safe.

Dinner is a macaroni and cheese from a box. Even though it's my favorite comfort food, I barely touch it. My nerves are completely shot by the time I go to bed for the night. I try to take comfort in the fact that Ransom is out there somewhere, watching. Even knowing I'm being looked after doesn't help me sleep. I toss and turn all night, waking up at three in the morning from a horrible nightmare. Colt was lying broken and bloodied with

Levi standing over him wearing his blood like a second skin.

There was no sleeping after that. It also solidified my decision to end things with Colt. I wouldn't be able to survive if something terrible happened to him because of me.

CHAPTER EIGHTEEN
Colt

I watch from afar as Darlene walks to school. Not being with her last night was hard. I want to wrap her up in my arms and keep her safe but staying away from her publicly is best for ending things quickly with Levi. He's out there somewhere, waiting. But then, so are we.

"She looks tired."

Ransom gives me a look that tells me I'm an idiot for stating the obvious. "Did you sleep like a baby last night?"

I snort. "I barely slept at all."

"Well, there you go."

"Smartass."

He chuckles. "This will all be over soon."

"I hope you're right."

As soon as Darlene is inside the school, I jump in my car and take a circuitous route to the school.

She's waiting in my office when I get there. Unexpected, but having her back in touching distance after a night fraught with worry is exactly what I need. I cross the room towards her, but she puts her arms out and takes a step back.

"What's wrong?"

Darlene shakes her head. "Colt, we can't do this anymore. People are talking. I can't take it. I knew this was a bad idea. I just can't."

My heart plummets. "Who's talking about us?"

"It doesn't matter. The fact that anyone is talking, judging me—you—for dating a coworker." She shakes her head sadly. "This has to end. It wasn't ever supposed to be more than a little fun at the club…"

"Bullshit," I growl. "This was never just going to be a bit of fun. You were mine from the moment I saw you in the club. We're made for each other…"

She lets out a deep sigh. "I'm sorry, Colt. I just can't."

Before I can respond, she turns and strides out of my office and into the hallway that's quickly filling with students, essentially making it impossible to follow her. If she thinks this conversation is over, she's mistaken. I refuse to give up on us just because some idiots are gossiping about us.

Three days.

It has been three days since Darlene broke things off with me and I'm going crazy. She refuses to have a conversation with me. She ignores all of my calls and my texts. Here at school, she's constantly with Melinda or one of the other teachers in the Fine Arts department. She's literally never alone. That is until she's walking either to the school or home from the school.

I've put every ounce of my willpower into not showing up at her apartment. Jasper and Ransom both told me that being apart is the best thing for catching Levi, only he hasn't shown his face yet. I hate that they are right. Knowing that Darlene is single—at least she thinks we are—gives him more opportunities to make his next move, whatever that may be.

I refuse to give up on her. She's my babygirl no matter what she thinks. Once this is all over with, I will be claiming what's mine.

CHAPTER NINETEEN
Darlene

I DIDN'T EXPECT Colt to give up on us so easily. It's a bitter pill to swallow, if I'm being honest. After those first three days, he stopped trying to corner me in the halls. All the phone calls and sweet texts about how much he misses me stopped too. It's as if we never were.

Even though it's what I asked for, it's not at all what I wanted. There haven't been any other threats from Levi, so I'm assuming he's somehow figured out that we aren't together anymore. I hate him a little more for keeping me from the man I now know I love desperately. It's just one more thing Levi Troy has taken from me. First, my sense of security and then my heart.

"Are you sure you don't want to go out?" Mel asks. "It might be good to get out of the house and stop moping about."

She's not wrong. I have been moping. I didn't tell her any details on why Colt and I broke up, but she's been fully supportive of me and has stood beside me while I cried. She's a good friend, and I'm lucky to have her.

I sigh. "I'm sorry I'm such a sad sack. You're right, I could use a night out. What should we do?"

"I could go for some of that pizza we had last time."

I smile the first genuine smile I've had for days. "Sounds like a plan. I could go for some of that greasy goodness. Maybe one of the triple chocolate chip cookie brownies too."

"What is this heaven you speak of?"

I laugh an all-out belly laugh at the look of wonder on her face. I lace my arm through hers and pull her along. "Come on. Let's go stuff our faces with pizza and brownies."

We opt to walk to the restaurant since it's not that far away. Mel keeps looking over her shoulder as we walk, and I wonder if she's picked up that I'm being followed. I debate on telling her but worry about how she will react.

"I feel like we are being followed," she leans in close and whispers.

I chew my lip and decide it's better to tell her than let her think someone is stalking us... Well, someone is stalking me, but I have a feeling the one she's talking about is either Ransom or Jasper, my two main protectors these days.

"We are... I mean... someone is following me. I'm sorry, I should've told you before. I actually... um... well, I sort of have a stalker. So I have someone that basically follows me everywhere, keeping an eye on me in case the person tries to attack me... or something." I cringe, waiting for her reaction.

"A stalker?! Oh, God. Why didn't you tell me? How long has this been going on? Do you know who it is?"

I let out a sigh, hating that I'm now involving my friend but also feeling glad to be talking to someone about it. "Mr. Troy..."

"Levi Troy?" she asks, shocked. "You know? I'm not that surprised. He was completely infatuated with you. More so than any of the other women he's bothered over the years."

"Well, it seems like he finally found someone to fixate on. Yay me." I try to put a little humor in my tone, but it's no use. Nothing about the situation is funny.

Mel shakes her head. "This is insane. And you have a bodyguard?"

I snort. "Try three... though I sort of suspect it's four."

Her eyes go wide. "Who?"

"Well, Jasper, the school patrol officer... when he's off the clock, he relieves Ransom. Do you know him? He's a good friend to Coach Cooper, Colt, and Jasper."

She shakes her head. "I don't think so. Who are the other two?"

I give her a wry smile wondering how she's going to feel about one of them, specifically Coach Cooper. "I think Colt has been watching over me despite our break up. I could be wrong, but I sometimes just feel like his eyes are on me. There's a weighted feel to how he looks at me. Maybe it's just wishful thinking.

"The other one is Coach Cooper. He watches out for me during the school day."

There's a flash of awareness in her eyes, maybe a little jealousy too. Both her and Coop have a serious attraction to each other, but for some reason, no one is making any moves. I have a good idea why Coop is keeping his distance. Coop is a daddy dom, and as far as he knows, Mel isn't a little. Though I think she could be... she has the disposition of a submissive for sure, and I don't think it's a far step for her to be a little. I think with a little coaching, she could be exactly what he needs.

Why she isn't asking him out is easier... she's shy. Ridiculously shy. The only time she isn't shy is when she's in front of her class or playing one of the many instruments she's trained in. I hate that they are missing out on what could be a wonderful relationship.

"And you really think that Colt is watching over you?" she asks, completely avoiding the topic of Cooper.

"I don't know. Like I said, maybe it's wishful thinking..."

We lapse into silence until we place our orders. Melinda starts to talk multiple times but remains silent.

"Just say it," I finally say, curiosity finally getting the better of me.

"Why did you and Colt break up?"

I collapse back against the booth and heave out a sigh. "Do you want the reason I told him or the whole truth?"

She gives me a bewildered look as if she can't believe there's more than one reason for my insanity. "Both."

"I told him it was because of all the other teachers who were judging me and that it was the exact reason I wanted to keep things quiet."

Melinda looks shocked. "No one was judging you! Everyone was just concerned after the attack."

I let out a dark laugh. "Yeah, I know that, but I very

well couldn't tell him the truth. He never would have accepted it."

"And the truth is..."

"I got a threat."

Her eyes widen in fear.

"A threat against Colt if I didn't break up with him. Levi is unhinged. He threatened to do something horrible to any obstacle in his path." I fight back the tears that want to fall every time I think about the possibility that Colt could be hurt because of me.

"Oh, Darlene. You should've just told Colt about the threat and let him make the choice himself."

I brush a lone tear that escapes as I choke back a sob. "He never would have let me leave him if he knew the real reason. I can't risk him."

Mel reaches across the table and holds my hand. "I understand, even if I don't agree. Colt is a big boy; he can take care of himself."

She's not wrong. It's just a risk I'm not prepared to take no matter how much sense it makes to tell him about the pictures and the threats. After that, our conversation moves to easier things. We talk about her Freshman students and how awful they are at keeping time. She even compares some of the woodwind players to dying birds. I laugh and feel lighter than I have in days.

I tell her about the horrible paintings my students are working on. We're recreating classics, and the art they are creating is tragic. She laughs when I tell her about the stick figure Mona Lisa. "I'm not joking. It's literally a stick figure with what the student describes as

Mona Lisa's smile. I can't tell if they are being serious or if it's a big joke to them."

She snorts her laugh, almost choking on her drink. "Stop it, you're going to kill me."

We both bust out in laughter again and it feels so good. I forgot how good it feels to just talk about normal things with a female friend. I've been sorely lacking in female companionship since I moved. The thought makes me miss my bestie. I wish that Charity was here to meet Melinda. They would totally get along.

After we finish eating, we head back to the school so that Melinda can get her car. It's dark outside and my anxiety sparks at having to walk home in the dark. I wonder who it is that's watching out for me tonight. I wave Mel off and my phone buzzes with a text.

The text is from Colt. My heart jumps into my throat when I read his message: *Just walk home like normal. He's watching.*

It takes a lot of self-control not to look around and see if I can see where Levi is watching from. Survival instinct is kicking in and I want to run home and lock myself inside my apartment and never leave again. I shove my phone into my back pocket and shrug my bag further up onto my shoulder, mentally preparing myself to walk the five blocks back to my apartment like I normally would.

My skin crawls as I make my way home. Thinking he might be watching me and knowing he's watching me are totally different. I thought I was afraid before, now I can hardly catch my breath knowing he's somewhere close. What's he going to do? Why now?

I make it home without incident. By the time I make

it inside and have my doors locked, my heart is pounding in my chest, and I can't seem to catch my breath. There's a knock on my door and I let out a little scream.

"It's me, Darlene." I feel an instant relief knowing that it's Colt on the other side of the door. I throw the locks open faster than ever before and open the door. I collapse into his arms, and he holds me close. "Shh, you're okay."

He lifts me in his arms and carries me to the couch. He sits with me on his lap and offers me his comfort. Selfishly, I soak it up. Drawing in his strength. He whispers sweet words to me, and I cry harder, knowing that his being here is putting him at risk.

"Did you catch him?" I ask through a shuddering breath.

He shakes his head. "The fucker got away," he growls lowly, sounding more menacing than even the most feral of animals.

Panic floods my system. If he got away, Colt can't be here. He's in danger. "You have to leave."

Hurt and confusion show on his face but are gone just as soon as they came making me wonder if I imagined it. "I can't do that, babygirl. I can't leave you tonight."

I shake my head, ready to argue, but I don't get the chance. "No matter if we aren't together, I can't stand being away. Levi got too close today. I won't leave you alone and vulnerable."

"But isn't that the point?"

"I don't fucking care what the point is. If you don't let me stay, I'll sit outside your door all night. I won't be able to rest if I don't know you're safe," he says in his stern daddy voice.

The voice that makes me melt inside. My heart pitter-patters in my chest knowing he still cares so much that he'd be willing to stay outside my door just to keep me safe. "You can stay, but it doesn't change anything."

"I know," he growls. "I'll stay on the couch. I just have to know you're safe."

I leave him with a blanket and pillow and head to bed myself. I can't sleep no matter how much I try. My mind won't stop focusing on what could possibly happen if Levi finds out that Colt is here. What if he makes good on his threats and hurts him?

The stress from the day bubbles up and out my eyes in the form of giant wracking sobs and ugly tears. Colt must hear me because the next thing I know, he's crawling into bed behind me and pulling me into his arms. My heart instantly feels lighter at being reunited. I let myself enjoy this stolen moment. I'm already taking a huge risk by letting Colt stay. I might as well go all in.

Thankfully I finally fall into a peaceful sleep. I sleep better than I have since this whole thing started knowing that I'm safe in the arms of the man I love. I can't help but worry about what happens next. How will I ever be strong enough to keep Colt at arm's length now?

CHAPTER TWENTY
Colt

EVEN WITH DARLENE safe in my arms, I can't seem to relax. All I can see is the look of panic on her face whenever I told her I was staying and that Levi wasn't caught. Why would she panic at knowing I'm here? Or was it just panic because Levi hasn't been caught yet, and it's not over? I can't shake the feeling that she's hiding something.

Could there be a different reason she doesn't want me around other than the one she gave me when she broke up with me? I'm not sure what's going on, but I will get to the bottom of it. I refuse to roll over and give up on Darlene. Once all of this is over, I'm going to do everything in my power to show her how much I love her.

It takes a long time for me to fall asleep. My sleep is plagued by nightmares of a broken and bloody Darlene. When morning comes, I feel like warmed-over garbage and am even more concerned about what Levi's end game is for Darlene.

I leave shortly after Darlene wakes up. She still has dark circles under her eyes even though her sleep was restful. She looks like she's got the weight of the world on her shoulders... maybe she does. I can't imagine how helpless she feels right now. Her life isn't her own anymore. She moves to a new city for a fresh start and a new job only to be stalked by a psycho and made to live in fear.

I walk across the street to where I know Ransom is watching Darlene's apartment building. I climb into his car and he hands me a coffee. "Did you get it out of your system?" he growls.

"Never. She'll never be out of my system. Knowing she's not safe will never sit well with me. I want to be by her side always."

"It's for the best, though. You know that," he says, arguing his point. "She's perfectly safe with me and the others watching over her. Not to mention your obsessed ass. From the outside looking in, you're more of a stalker than Levi at this point."

"Fuck off. Do we know where Levi ran off to?" I ask, unable to hide my anger and frustration at the fact that he eluded us last night.

Ransom shakes his head. "Not a clue. He ducked between two buildings, and it was like he just melted into the shadows."

"How did he just fucking disappear like that? He's way more of a problem than we originally thought."

Ransom lets out a low growl. "Darlene isn't his first victim." He pulls out a folder and hands it to me. "I did some more digging last night and found out that Levi Troy didn't exist until five years ago."

"That's just before he started working at Thurston Academy."

He nods. "Yep. It seems that Mr. Levi Troy used to be one Leonard Trey. Leonard has multiple restraining orders filed against him, not to mention that he's currently wanted for assault. It seems that he attacked his last victim—nearly killed her."

Rage bubbles up inside my core; right alongside that is fear. Fear for the woman I love. Now we know exactly what Levi—Leonard—is capable of, and I don't like it one little bit. I feel the need to rush back to Darlene's side and never leave. Ransom has a point about leaving her seemingly alone, though. Someone like Levi isn't likely to attack when there's another man around.

"Keep close to her. I don't want that fucker laying on finger on her."

Ransom snorts. "You know I'm a professional, right?"

"I don't care if you've guarded the president. Darlene is far more precious."

I hop out of Ransom's car and head to my own. Time to go get ready for work. It's a struggle to not go back up to Darlene's apartment and force her to let me take care of her. Somehow, I manage.

CHAPTER TWENTY-ONE

Darlene

I'M EXHAUSTED EVEN though I slept peacefully in Colt's arms last night. It wasn't nearly enough to catch up on all the missed sleep from this week. Add all the stress and high anxiety days to the sleepless nights, and you get one tired girl. I'm drained. Completely and totally drained.

School drags. It feels like the day is never-ending, and all I want to do is go home and soak in the tub and pretend that life is normal again. I'm feeling every bit of the stress that I've been trying to ignore.

Deciding to be a bit of a rebel, I release my last class of the day early. It only takes me a moment to collect all of my things. The second the final bell for the day rings, I am out the door and heading home.

My phone buzzes in my purse when I'm about halfway home. I pull it out and notice several missed calls and a few texts, all from Colt.

Jasper needs to talk to you.
Don't leave the school on your own.

Wait for someone to walk with you...
Darlene?

A fission of fear fills me with dread. Half of me wants to turn and run back to the school. The other half wants to run the rest of the way home and to the safety of my apartment.

I left already. Halfway home. I respond.

I scream, and my phone goes flying to the ground when someone grabs me from inside the alley I'm walking past. I fight, but the person is bigger and stronger than me. The smell of body odor and stale cigarette smoke makes me gag, but I fight even harder.

"No one watching the pretty-pretty princess today?" the voice snarls—Levi.

I knew this moment was coming. I mean, this is why I was walking alone to begin with, right? I was staying away from Colt so that I could be the bait. What does Levi mean that no one is watching me? Someone is always watching—fear spikes through me at the idea that I'm alone.

"Let me go!" I scream, flailing my legs and yanking against his hold. No matter what I do, it doesn't seem to work. I fling my head back and make contact with something... his nose, maybe? Because he screams and shoves me away and against a brick wall.

My hands scrape on the rough surface, but I ignore that small pain and take off towards the sidewalk and help. I only make it three steps before he's on me again. This time he pins me to the wall, and I see a flash of silver as he pulls a knife from somewhere and holds it to my throat.

"Don't be a tease. I've waited for this for too long

already."

I stand stock-still, not knowing what to do now that there's a knife to me. All of the self-defense classes I took in college failed to cover knives to throats. Jesus.

What do I do?
What do I do?

I repeat the question to myself, feeling more and more out of control with each passing second. How am I going to get out of this? Where is Ransom? He's always watching. What if Levi is right and no one is watching? I could be nothing but a bloody body on the ground after all of this—a corpse for someone to find.

Levi leans in and licks the side of my face. I gag, barely holding back my vomit as his fetid breath fills my senses. "Mm almost as good as I thought," he says manically.

"Please, Levi. You don't have to do this," I beg.

"I tried to do it the right way. I asked you out! Would you give me a chance? No! You'd rather spread your whore legs for Colton Fucking James. Mister perfect principal that everyone likes."

I gasp as the knife pricks my skin with his rising ire.

"Look what you made me do!" he yells in my face. His eyes fall to the place on my neck where I can feel blood trickling from the small cut he just made. There is an unhinged quality to the way he's staring at my blood, almost like he wants more. It scares me worse than anything else could. He isn't just obsessed to the point of wanting to keep me or make me his... I'm starting to think he's obsessed to the point of killing me.

I'm starting to panic now. I can't get the image of my broken body on the dirty alley ground out of my head.

My breaths are coming in short pants, and darkness starts to creep in on the edges of my vision. I realize I'm close to passing out. I can't do that. I have to focus. I have to figure out how to get out of this.

Levi presses against me, and I cringe back as much as I can, which isn't much at all since I'm practically pinned to the wall. He leans forward, his lips descending on mine. I turn my head as much as I can without hurting myself on the knife. Just before his lips make contact, there is a roar at the mouth of the alley. Levi jumps back just as a dark figure tackles him to the ground.

"Colt!" I shout. "He has a knife!"

It all happens so fast. One minute Levi has a knife to my throat, and in the next, Colt has that same knife against Levi's. Levi doesn't stop fighting. At one point, I think he's going to buck Colt off of him, but then Colt slams his fist into his face, and Levi goes limp, knocked out cold.

Colt tosses the knife aside and rushes to my side. "Are you okay, baby?" He looks me up and down, taking in the small nick on my neck. His hands cup my cheeks, and he looks me in the eye. "Please, talk to me, Darlene. Are you hurt?"

"Jus-sst scared."

He lightly touches my neck below my injury. "And this. Did he touch you?" he asks with a low, menacing growl.

I shake my head, no. "He... he licked me," I stutter out. "My cheek..."

Colt snarls and moves to leave me. I panic and grab ahold of him. "D-don't leave me."

His tense muscles instantly relax, and he holds me

tight. "I'm not going anywhere, Darlene."

"Colt!?" I hear someone shouting from the street. Jasper, maybe.

"Here," Colt hollers back.

"Jesus," Jasper says, taking in Levi's prone form laying on the ground in a broken heap. "Is he alive?"

My eyes widen at that. Surely a single punch wouldn't kill someone as large as Levi Troy...

"Unfortunately," Colt says, sounding remorseful that he didn't kill the man. "He deserves to die."

"As your friend, I'm going to agree. As a cop, I'm going to pretend I didn't hear that," he says. "You okay, sweetheart?"

I nod, still clinging to Colt.

Jasper makes a couple phone calls, and before I know it, the alley is filled with police and detectives. I give my statement what feels like ten times until Colt has had enough and tells them all he's taking me home. I'm eternally grateful that he's taking charge. I'm overwhelmed and can't handle anymore.

Colt leads me away from the scene of the attack, and I'm doubtful I will ever be able to walk to and from school again. Looks like my aging car is going to get more miles on it. I barely make it four steps before I trip on my own feet. A sob breaks free, and if Colt wasn't here to catch me, I would've fallen to my knees. Everything hits me at once. The attack, the millions of questions from the police making me relive the moment over and over, the fact that it's over... it all comes crashing down, and I suddenly can't breathe.

Colt holds me up and tips my face up to his. Icy blue eyes meet mine, giving me something to focus on.

"Breathe, Darlene. Take a deep breath in…" My breath stutters into my lungs, then gusts out on another sob. "Shh. It's okay, babygirl. Just breathe."

I take in another breath and another until the darkness at the edges of my vision goes away, and I'm no longer hyperventilating. "Good girl," Colt praises. "Just breathe with me."

I nod my head, following his breathing pattern. In… out… over and over until I'm feeling calmer. "Th-thanks," I stutter out.

"Let's get you home."

I turn to walk towards home, and Colt grabs me up, lifting me into his arms. Once again, I'm caught off guard by his strength. I let out a feeble protest that he completely ignores. I wrap my arms around his neck and cling to that strength of his, loving how safe I feel in his arms.

He sets me down outside my apartment door. He takes my keys from me and opens the door. As soon as the door is shut and locked, he lifts me back up and carries me to the couch. I don't realize I'm shaking until Colt wraps me up in a throw blanket.

"It's okay, babygirl. You're safe now," he promises.

He disappears into the kitchen and comes back with my sneaky box of truffles and a bottle of water. He opens the water and indicates I need to drink. Without thought, I take the water and gulp it down. Then he hands me a truffle and tells me to eat, that the sugar will help. I take a nibble, then another. He's right that the water and chocolate are helping me feel steadier.

"Thanks." I take a deep calming breath and feel more myself. Except I feel dirty. I can still feel Levi's hands on me, his tongue... I gag. I barely make it to the bathroom before I vomit. Colt is right there, holding my hair and rubbing soothing circles on my back.

"Shh... It's okay, Darlene."

"Dirty," I whimper between retches.

Realization comes over him, and he instantly turns on the shower. I feel immensely grateful for this man taking care of me even though it's not his job anymore. I broke us, and yet, here he is. He goes to leave me to my shower, but I grab his arm. "Stay, please," I beg, not wanting to be alone.

"Are you sure?"

"Yes. I don't want to be alone yet."

"Okay, babygirl." He reaches to cup my cheek, and I flinch away, not wanting him to touch me where Levi did. His arm drops, and a look of hurt crosses his features before he shutters it. Not thinking, I grab his other hand and hold it to my opposite, unsullied cheek. Realization dawns on him, and he gently touches the clean side of my face.

When he steps away, I carefully undress, dumping my clothes on the floor. I will never wear those again. In fact, I may just burn them. Colt watches me in a clinical way, making sure that I'm steady on my feet, not with any of the lust he normally would have. I'm thankful for that.

The first thing I do in the shower is scrub my face. Again, and again. I hiss when I wash my arms, I look at my elbows, seeing where the brick abraded them. Colt is instantly there, lifting my arm and looking at the angry red skin.

"Baby, why didn't you tell me you were hurt?"

"I didn't realize..." I sniffle.

"It's okay. Finish your shower. I'll get some cream for that."

I do as requested and finish washing. I wash every inch of my body more than once and still don't feel completely clean. I wash my hair twice, then my face again. Colt hands me one of my oversized towels. I dry off and wrap it around my body. Tears prick my eyes as Colt carefully towel dries my hair for me just like a daddy dom would for his babygirl. Only... he's not my daddy anymore because I ruined that.

He then carefully puts some antibacterial ointment on my scrapes and leads me to my bedroom, where he's laid out a set of comfy pajamas. He goes to the door to give me privacy to dress, and I whimper at the thought of him leaving me. I don't know why I'm feeling clingy. It's not fair to him. Not when I broke things off.

Even though I don't want him to be out of my sight, I let him leave without protest. I dress quickly and follow him out of the room. Only I don't find him in the living room. He's in my studio looking at my most recent project.

I chew on my lip, wondering what he thinks of the painting. It's us... well, a representation of us done in a more abstract style than my typical realism. It hurt too much to paint us as we are—were. I clear my throat so he knows I'm here and he turns, looking at me with curious eyes.

"Is this us?"

I could easily say no, but I'm not a liar. "Yes..."

"It's beautiful."

My cheeks heat with a blush knowing that he likes

my painting. Thoughts of Levi are long gone as I watch Colt look at my painting with awe. This room is my escape from the world at large so it's easy to forget everything that has happened today.

"I've missed you." The words escape my mouth before I can stop them. It's not fair of me. Not when I'm the one who broke us to begin with. Sure, Levi was the catalyst, but I'm the one that made the choice to end things instead of telling Colt about the threats against him. "Sorry, I shouldn't have said that."

He turns to me and gives me a knowing look. "You didn't break things off with me because of rumors, did you?"

Shock jolts through me at his assessment of the situation. He's completely right about it, but how does he know? "I..."

He crosses the room to me and hugs me. "It's okay, baby, you can tell me."

Now it's decision time. Do I stick to the lie, or do I confess? "Levi threatened you. He promised to hurt you if I didn't break things off. I couldn't risk you... I lo-" I barely stop myself before I profess my love for him. "I care about you too much for that."

"Darlene... You should have told me. I knew about the threats. He had dozens of pictures of me with my face burned or slashed through on his walls. It was pretty apparent that he didn't like us together."

Shock reverberates inside me. Of course. I remember seeing the pictures from his house. The shrine to me and the threatening pictures where he'd ruined or ripped Colt out of them. Why didn't I remember that at the time?

Because I was panicked. Scared because it all became so real. Bad excuses, but that's the only reason I can think that would have made me forget the fact that Colt was already in danger because of me.

"I'm... I didn't..." I shake my head at a loss for words.

"It's okay. I know you had my best interests at heart. Just... next time talk to me, okay?"

"Next time?" I ask, hopefully. "Will there be a next time?"

"Well, not the stalker part, I hope," he says, trying to insert a little humor into the situation. "I want to be with you, Darlene. That's all I've ever wanted."

I look at him with equal parts shock and happiness. "But-"

"There are no buts, babygirl. You're everything I've ever wanted. We're perfect together. You're my other half," he proudly professes. "Unless that's not what you want."

Tears stream down my cheeks, this time, they are one hundred percent happy. "I do. I want you, Colt."

"Then, you have me."

I fall against his chest and hug him tight. I almost confess my love, but don't want those words to be tied to this day. Yes, it's brought me back to Colt, but it also has so much negativity. Those words deserve to have their own day. Their own moment.

He holds me for a long time before we finally break apart. He sets me up on the couch, once again wrapped up in a blanket, only this time he turns on my favorite baking show and goes to the kitchen. A few minutes later, he comes back with an omelet that smells divine.

"Thanks," I say around a bite of cheesy goodness. I

devour the entire thing, not having realized how hungry I was.

"You're welcome, beauty. Are you feeling better?"

I sigh. "Yeah. I think so. Still kind of shaken."

"It'll take time. Do you want to talk about it?"

I snort a sardonic laugh. "I think I've talked about it enough for one day."

"Yeah, I guess so," he says with a sad smile. "I'm here if you need to talk. No pressure."

"Thanks, Colt." I have to fight the desire to call him daddy. I don't deserve that privilege, not yet. After breaking up with him like I did, I definitely need to earn that right back. I need to prove to him that I can be a good little girl for him.

"No need to thank me, that's what I'm here for."

My response is cut off by a jaw-popping yawn. "I don't know why I'm so tired."

"You've had a big day. Why don't we get you into bed?"

He reaches out a hand to me, which I don't hesitate to take and let him lead me towards my bedroom. He lovingly tucks me into the bed, and I relax into the cool sheets. He goes to leave, but I reach out to him and ask him to stay.

He climbs into bed beside me, completely dressed. I roll over and rest my head over his heart, loving the sound of the strong, steady beat under my ear. I draw comfort from having him so close. It doesn't take long for sleep to claim me. I thought my sleep would be plagued by nightmares, but I sleep peacefully.

CHAPTER TWENTY-TWO
Darlene

I WAKE up alone and my heart falls until I hear Colt in the other room. It sounds like he's in the kitchen. I stretch and climb out of bed feeling rested for the first time in days. Maybe because I'm waking up for the first time in weeks without anxiety. The stress and foreboding of someone out there stalking me was a heavy burden to bear. And, like an idiot, I let myself bear it alone instead of just talking to Colt.

I find Colt in the kitchen like I suspected and blush when I realize he's unpacking the last of my boxes that I still haven't gotten to. "You don't have to do that," I say even though I am feeling beyond grateful because I hate unpacking.

"Have to, no. Want to, yes."

He puts down the pan he's holding and comes over to me for a hug. I wrap my arms around him, soaking up his strength. I rest my chin on his chest and look up at him. "Thank you..." I almost call him daddy again but know that it's not time yet. He's not made any indication that we are back to normal, and I don't want to push it.

"You're welcome, beauty. You deserve to feel like you fully live here. It's been months, and you're still living out of boxes."

I shrug. "My studio and bedroom are all I need." I scrunch up my nose, looking at the kitchen. "I don't cook so most of that is superfluous anyway."

He chuckles. "I do cook, though."

I quirk up an eyebrow at that. Does that mean he's going to be spending a lot of time here? Not that I have any arguments with that. I love having him here. Though why he would choose my small apartment compared to his house, I have no idea.

"One of us has to, and if you leave it up to me, it'll be marshmallow cereal and yogurt three meals a day."

He lightly tickles my side. "Not on my watch..."

I giggle, the sound foreign to my own ears. When was the last time I felt free to laugh and be silly? My little side has been shoved into the corner of my mind for so long it feels good to let her stretch her legs so to speak.

"Why don't you go take a shower while I finish up this last box, and we can watch a movie."

I beam up at him. "Can we watch *Legend*?"

"You bet."

"Tom Cruise is so cute in that one!" I say, dancing towards the bathroom, but not before Colt gives me a light love tap on my bottom in warning for my snark.

It's been two days of cuddling on the couch watching movies and Colt hasn't so much as kissed me with anything other than platonic affection. He talked me into taking the week off to recuperate after the attack. I easily agreed once he agreed to take the week off too. Now it's Sunday afternoon, and he's leaving to get a bag of clothes and things from his place.

He gives me a sweet kiss on the top of my head before leaving, and I flop back on the couch in frustration. I love that Colt is doting on me and basically spoiling me rotten, but I hate that he's treating me like I'm going to crack into a million pieces at the slightest thing.

Yes, what happened Friday was traumatic, and no, I'm not over it—I won't be for a long while, I suspect—but it has nothing to do with Colt and me. I love all the cuddles. I really do. I want more than just that though. He won't even give me more than a PG-rated kiss. I've been without him for weeks, and it's driving me crazy to have him here but only part of him.

I'm happy he agreed to take the week off with me. I'm hoping it will give us a chance to reconnect. I've hinted at wanting to get back to our daddy and little relationship, but he's either being obtuse about it or doesn't want to dive back into it. I miss it. I need the freedom and discipline that comes with being Colt's babygirl.

While Colt is gone, I make the best of my time. I want to make it clear that I'm ready to resume our relationship—our whole relationship. I decide to just go all in. I find a pretty dress like what I would wear to the club and put it on. Nerves start creeping in because I'm being extremely forward and wouldn't handle being rejected well at all.

"He won't reject me," I say aloud to the room. "He's just being overly careful because of my trauma..."

I hope.

Not sure how to coax Colt into picking up where we left off, I decide to go to my studio. It's the place where I think the best. Maybe inspiration will spark. Ugh. The room is a disaster. I've been so distraught these last several weeks that I haven't been cleaning up. I've just let things fall where they may. I decide to tidy up while I wait for something to come to me.

I'm humming my favorite song and cleaning my drawing table when I hear the door open and close—a thrill of excitement courses through me knowing that Colt is back. I look down at the ruler I was just getting ready to put away when that inspiration I was looking for strikes...

"Darlene?" Colt calls from the other room.

"In the studio!"

I hear his heavy footfalls as he makes his way towards me and my insane idea...

CHAPTER TWENTY-THREE

Colt

I WALK into the room and see Darlene bent over her desk, rearranging something. I groan internally because not only has she changed into one of her pretty dresses that she wears when she's feeling like her little self but because it's short enough to show off her panty covered ass when she bends over.

Pure fucking torture.

I've been so careful with her these past couple of days. All I can see is the traumatized woman from the alley. Bleeding from a cut on her neck and pale as a ghost. I can't get the vision out of my head. Every time I think about it, I get sick to my stomach and can't stand the idea of rushing her back into a relationship where she gives up her control.

Now I'm wondering if that was the right move or not because from the looks of things, she's telling me she's ready and willing to restart our dynamic.

"What are you up to, Darlene?" I ask, even though I know exactly what she's doing.

"I'm just tidying up." She turns and gives me a mischievous look telling me that's definitely not all she's up to.

Darlene stands up straight and turns around, holding her hands behind her back. She gives me a smile that says she's sweet and innocent, but the spark in her eyes says something altogether different.

"You look beautiful, babygirl."

Her cheeks flush pink at my compliment. She's always been so confident that it's strange seeing her so shy. Does she think I'm going to reject her? Perhaps I've read the whole situation wrong. She didn't need me to handle her with such care as a man would the woman he loves after something so traumatic.

She's needed me to be her daddy. Strong and confident. Taking charge and leading the way instead of letting her lead. I won't make that mistake again. If she needs me to be her daddy, that's exactly what I will give her. Seeing the light on in her eyes again is enough to tell me my new course of action is the right one.

Darlene comes towards me, that mischievous smile spreading wide as she closes the distance between us. She stops short, rocking back on her feet with her hands still behind her back.

"What do you think you're doing, babygirl?" I growl.

A playful glint shines from her big brown eyes as she circles around me. "Nothing, daddy," she singsongs.

She's lying, and she's terrible at it, but I like that she's lost the hunted look she's had for weeks now. Being reunited after being apart so long feels right. This is the first time since she pushed me away that I've felt complete. I stand in place, turning my head and watching as she circles me. She's just shy of arm's length, or I'd already have her in my arms. I'm too curious as to what she thinks she's up to... and what she has hidden behind her back.

On her second pass, she dashes forward, and something cracks down on my ass. My eyes go wide at the impetuousness of my little girl spanking me. She drops the implement and darts out of the room, taking off to somewhere else in her apartment. I look down and smirk at the discarded ruler on the floor.

Game on.

I pick up the ruler and stroll out of the room after my babygirl and her soon to be bright red ass.

CHAPTER TWENTY-FOUR
Darlene

I FEEL LIGHTER than I have in weeks. Pushing Colt away cracked a fissure in my heart a mile wide. It was so hard having him right there in front of me day after day and not being able to touch him. I shake my head at my stupidity and cowardice. It took me way too long to see how wrong I was to push him away without telling him why.

Colt is the only man I want. The only person in the world who is the daddy counterpart to my little girl. When I think about the future, I can't see anyone else—only him. The man who is slowly stalking me through my apartment as I rush to hide from his wrath.

He's been careful with me, but what he hasn't realized is that's not what I need. I need him to make things right between us again. The only way for me to feel that things are back on even ground is to repent for breaking us without an honest reason as to why. Now I've thrown a red flag in front of the bull by spanking him with a ruler. I knew exactly what I was doing. What I was asking for.

I want... no, I *need* the punishment. I need him to absolve me of the guilt I've been harboring since the day I pushed him away. I think we both need the fresh start. I stand in the middle of my living room, spinning circles looking for a place to hide—of course there isn't any. It's merely adrenaline that's causing me to look in the first place. I don't really want to hide. I want to be caught. I want Colt's hands on me. To be under his control, at complete mercy to his every whim.

He strides into the room, looking like an Adonis, even without the normal suit and tie. His strong jaw and icy eyes make my stomach swoop. He's so sexy I want to fall to my knees and worship him. A smirk twitches at the corner of his lips as he watches me watch him. He knows exactly what he does to me, and he loves it.

I stand in the middle of the room, frozen. Without a word, he strips off his jacket and tosses it over the back of a chair. I whimper when he slowly starts to roll his shirtsleeves up to his elbows. Arm porn is a real thing. I don't know what it is about seeing a stern man rolling his sleeves up that gets me going, but it so does.

He reaches behind him and pulls the ruler from his back pocket. *Oh crap.* Definitely in trouble for my little stunt. The heated way Colt is looking at me makes it worth it though. He was all cautious touches and sweet cuddles as if he thought I was a wounded rabbit ready to hop away at the slightest provocation. This is me telling him to stop handling me with kid gloves.

"Come here, babygirl," Colt commands gruffly.

I shiver at the heat in his tone. I slowly close the

distance between us, just slow enough to add to my impudence—his jaw ticks. I can tell he's trying to hold back his amusement. He's not even a little angry or disappointed like he's trying to act so his façade keeps slipping.

When I'm directly in front of him, I smile up at him brightly. "Hi, daddy. How can I help you?"

Colt snorts a laugh, his mask of sternness completely falling for a second before he pulls it back into place. "You've been a naughty girl..."

I blink up at him with mock surprise at his accusation. "Not me, daddy. I'm your good girl. Must be some other little girl."

He raises a brow and reaches out to pull me into him. "There's only one little girl for me. Darlene, you're it. Forever."

I swoon into him at his declaration. It's not the 'I love you' I am waiting for, but it's darn close. "Forever is a long time..."

He growls, wrapping his fist in my hair, tilting my head back so there's nowhere for me to look but in his eyes. "Forever isn't long enough for how much I love you, Darlene."

Oh, wow. He said it. I mean... he actually said the words. Before I have a chance to say them back, Colt has his lips crushed to mine in a life-altering kiss. The kiss breaks me into a million tiny pieces and knits me back together again, wholly changed. I lick my lips when he breaks the kiss, my eyes still closed as I savor the lasting effects of his lips on mine.

My eyes slowly blink open, and I'm met with the hungry gaze of the man who just declared his love for me. "I love you, Colt... daddy... so much. I'm sorry I pushed-"

He steals away my words in another kiss, obviously not wanting to hear any more apologies. Which is fine with me. I'll show him how sorry I am by giving him everything he wants from me.

"You're so fucking beautiful, Darlene," he growls. "I want to bury myself inside you so deep you'll feel me for days."

I gasp nodding. "Yes, please."

He chuckles darkly, cracking the ruler down on my bottom. I forgot all about the ruler. That's what Colt does to me. He makes me forget everything. Including my impulsive nature writing a check my booty now has to cash. A little thrill of excitement rushes through me at the idea of being turned over his knee and spanked like the naughty girl I am.

"First, we need to discuss a few things." His tone is stern and a little dark. My butt muscles clench automatically at the threat in his words. "Strip."

I don't hesitate to reach behind me and slowly start tugging down the zipper on my dress. The dress gapes, making it easy to slip out of it. It pools around my ankles, leaving me in a pale green bra and panty set. They are far from sexy. Just plain cotton, but with the way Colt's looking at me, you would think I was wearing silk and lace. I reach behind me and unclasp my bra, letting it hit the floor with my dress. I step out of my panties and stand before him, completely bare. His hungry eyes rove over my nakedness like a caress.

He reaches out and rubs his thumb over my nipple, causing it to furl into a stiff peak. "So responsive." He does the same to the other nipple. My head drops back on a moan as he teases my nipples. His lips trail lightly over my neck as his hands grip my ass in an almost punishing grasp. I gasp and moan, loving his possessive touches.

Unable to help myself, I start to unbutton his shirt. I've only released three buttons when his strong hands grip my wrists, stopping me.

"Daddy," I plead. "I want to see you. To feel you."

"Soon, babygirl," he coos, then leads me towards the couch. He sits and pats his lap wordlessly telling me exactly what he wants. I don't even pretend to fight it. I want this as badly as he does.

I carefully arrange myself over his lap. I tense as I get into position. No matter how much I want the spanking, there is always that brief moment of fear of the unknown. How many spanks? How hard? Will it hurt? How bad will it hurt? I jump when his big hand comes down on my bottom in a gentle tap.

"Shh, relax, babygirl."

I inwardly snort. *Easy for you to say, you're not the one about to get their butt lit up.*

He caresses my skin, running soothing fingers up and down my back, drawing patterns on my skin until I'm completely limp over his lap. Only when I'm utterly relaxed, and my mind is quiet does the spanking start.

His hand comes down on my bottom over and over, not hard enough to really hurt. No, he's got other plans so he's just warming my skin. Preparing me for something harsher. I whimper when the hits come harder and faster, especially when he gets my sensitive sit spots.

Colt alternates spanking with rubbing until I'm so

lost to the bliss of it all that I'm floating in a haze of pleasurable pain. I'm jerked from that place in a second when the ruler cracks down on me in two quick slaps.

"Ow! Daddy!" I cry out more from shock than pain. He doesn't stop, despite my flailing legs. With a hand on my lower back, he pins me to his lap and continues my punishment.

"Do you know why you're getting this spanking?" he asks lowly.

"Because I spanked you with the ruler." That's not why, and I know it, but it's much easier than admitting that I pushed him away and caused us both unnecessary pain. Especially when I could have told him what was happening and prevented it all. The ruler cracks down directly on my sit spot, causing me to squeal. "Because I pushed you away!"

"Better. This spanking is to remind you that I'm your daddy. I'm yours, and only yours. And you are mine." He punctuates those last four words with a solid spank to each of my cheeks.

My whole bottom feels like it's on fire as my spanking commences. I'm crying and blubbering about how sorry I am and how much I love him and that I'll never leave him again when I hear the ruler fall to the hardwood floor. Colt pulls me up onto his lap, cuddling me.

"Shh... It's okay, beauty. All is forgiven now."

I wrap myself around his strong body, holding him close as he strokes his fingers through my hair. My freshly spanked bottom chafes against his jeans, reminding me of my punishment. His other hand slowly roams over my body, igniting my desire. He tweaks a nipple and I moan, wriggling against his hard length.

He fists my hair and pulls my lips up for a demanding kiss. A kiss that marks me as his more than any spanking ever could.

"Mine," he growls against my lips, his teeth nipping, his tongue stroking until we are both panting and moving against each other for the sweet friction we both crave. "I wanted to go slow, but I can't. I need you too fucking bad, Darlene."

"I'm yours, Colt. Take me. Fuck me," I demand with a little growl of my own. My hands fisting in his hair.

I gasp when he sweeps me off his lap and throws me over his shoulder. He storms down the hallway to my bedroom like a man on a mission. He tosses me onto the bed then rips his shirt off. Next come his pants and briefs. He stands before me completely naked and glorious. I want to kiss and lick every inch of his muscular chest down to his throbbing cock, but I know that's not happening right now.

Later, I think to myself. *Definitely later.*

Colt grabs my ankles and yanks me down to the edge of the bed. I gasp, then moan when his mouth comes down on me. He licks and sucks my clit, two of his thick fingers plunging inside me. His tongue swirls while his fingers work magic on my g-spot, and faster than I ever thought possible, I'm coming. He growls into my pussy, not letting up on his suckling. My orgasm crests, and then I'm thrown right into a second, more powerful one.

"Colt!" I scream, fisting his hair. I'm desperately pulling at him. I want him to stop. I want him to never stop. It's so good it hurts. My whole body is a confused mess of sensation. One part undeniable pleasure. The other exquisite pain. They bleed into one another until all I can do is scream out my orgasm.

Finally, he has mercy and releases my clit from his torment. "You taste like the sweetest candy," Colt rumbles. "I could eat you all day."

"You'd kill me," I say, panting for breath.

"You'd love it," he counters.

He's not wrong. What a sweet way to go. Death by orgasm.

Colt stands, his rock-hard cock thick and proud. "I'm going to fuck you now, beauty."

"Yes," I nod, wanting him as badly as he wants me.

Despite his declarations that he can't go slow, he inches his fat cock slowly into me until every bit of him is buried deep. He swivels his hips and I lose my mind at the feel of him grinding against my ultra-sensitive clit. He retreats from my body just as achingly slow. Then, with a look of fire in his eyes, he plunges back inside me. He fucks me deep and hard, losing every bit of the polished man he is and giving himself over to the baser part of himself. The part that needs to own me. To fuck me until he's claimed me fully.

"Daddy! Colt!" I chant his name over and over as he bottoms out on each inward thrust. Such exquisite torture every time he hits that spot deep inside that no one's ever touched before.

Without warning, my orgasm slams into me. I arch off the bed, clawing at my own hair. The bite of pain brings me higher. Colt slips his finger between us, rubbing firm circles around my clit.

"That's it, naughty girl. Come all over my cock." He

growls, the words hardly sounding human. "Fuck! I'm going to fill this tight little cunt with my come. Ruin you for all others. Mine," he snarls.

"Yours," I gasp, shaking my head in assent. "All yours, daddy."

With a groan, Colt buries himself to the hilt, and I feel his cock jump inside me. It pulses against my walls as his hot come floods my pussy. He pulls out and thrusts, again and again, spurt after spurt filling me until it's dripping from my clenching pussy.

Finally spent, he collapses on top of me, holding me in his strong arms. I wrap my arms and shaking legs around him. I love his weight on me—the connection—I never want him to leave. I want him to stay inside me, on top of me, claiming me.

He pulls from my depths and arranges my limp body against the pillows. He walks to the bathroom, and I hear running water. He comes back with a warm cloth and gently cleans my well-fucked pussy. I shudder when the cloth rasps over my sensitive button, each nerve ending prickling from the sensation.

Colt tosses the washcloth away and crawls onto the bed beside me, pulling me into his strong arms. He presses a firm kiss to the top of my head. "I love you, Darlene."

"I love you too, Colt—daddy. So much."

Safe in my daddy's arms, I fall into a peaceful knowing that everything is going to be okay.

EPILOGUE
Darlene—One Month Later

"You're just being stubborn now!" I say indignantly. I swear my best friend is the hardest person to convince to do what's best for her ever. "Come on, Cha-cha. Thurston needs a new cheer coach. Our current one just found out she's pregnant and is quitting at the end of the school year! It's perfect. You could be close to me and you've got family not too far away."

Charity snorts. "That is totally not a big bonus. In fact, being closer to Dale is about the biggest deterrent there is."

I mean, I can't really blame her for that her stepdad is a giant douche, but he's the only family she has left after her mom died from cancer ten years ago.

"It's a great opportunity..." I add, trying to get her away from thinking about being closer to her stepdad. Definitely shouldn't have mentioned him. Darn it.

"Okay, okay," she relents. "I'll send in my resume. But I'm not leaving Colson until the semester is up."

"That's perfect! The job starts for summer camp," I say excitedly.

Charity laughs. "It will be nice to see you every day again."

"I know. I've missed you. You'll love it here."

"I don't have the job yet," she warns. "Don't get your hopes up too high."

I snort a laugh at that one. "I'm pretty sure you'll be top of the list."

Colt pokes me in the side and gives me a look. Whoops. Guess I shouldn't be promising favors to be called in. That's sort of the exact reason I didn't want people to know we are together in the first place.

Oh well, I think shamelessly. I'll do anything to have my bestie here with me.

"Don't pull any strings, Darlene," Charity warns.

"Please, as if I need to do that. You're the best person for the job."

"You're too much." I can practically hear her rolling her eyes at me.

"But you love me."

"You know it. You better get going. You're going to miss your own party."

"It's called fashionably late."

Charity laughs. "You hate being late. Happy Birthday! I love you. Tell Colt hi for me."

"Will do! Love you most."

I hang up the phone with a smile. I can't wait until Charity moves here. Life will be absolutely perfect once she's here with me. A man I love, and that loves me, a job I love, a fun and safe club to play at, new friends, and soon my bestie. Yep. Life is good.

Colt comes back into the room and gives me a look that promises naughty things. "Are you finished meddling?"

"I'm just trying to help you out. You know you need a new girls' gym coach and cheer coach."

He gives me a knowing look. "And you miss your best friend."

I pout and nod. "And I miss my friend."

Colt shakes his head, laughing. "Come here, babygirl." I cross the room to where he's standing in his charcoal gray suit looking every bit the sexy principal he is. He pulls me into his arms and gives me a tender kiss. "I love you, Darlene."

"I love you, too, daddy."

"Are you ready to go to the club?"

I dance a little in excitement. "Yes! I'm so excited to see everyone."

He gives me another look. "Because you're excited about more meddling."

I gasp, holding a hand to my chest. "Moi? Meddle? Never."

"That's why you picked the club to have your birthday celebration at and invited Melinda?"

I mean, he's not completely wrong. But the real reason is that I love the restaurant at the club and am hoping for some playtime after dinner.

We get to the club and enter through the restaurant entrance instead of through the club proper. Everyone is already here, including Melinda, who is looking around at everyone in the restaurant with an incredulous expression on her face as if she's trying to solve a problem. Nothing looks outlandishly different than at a regular restaurant, but some of the couples definitely have a certain... flair to them. I choke back a giggle at seeing Coop standing closer than he usually does, giving anyone who looks at her threatening looks. He's got the air of an angry junkyard dog ready to attack if anyone dares come close to his fence.

Perfect.

I had a little bitty bit of hope that bringing Mel here would give Coop the nudge he obviously needs to make the next move. Since Mel is definitely too shy to initiate anything, even if she really wants to. I have a whole plan to matchmake, but from the looks of things, there might not be any need. Coop looks like he's ready to pee a circle around her to make sure no one else comes too close.

Tessa is the first to see us and she excitedly pops up from the chair she was waiting at and runs over. She throws her arms around me and hugs me close. "Happy birthday!"

"Thanks," I say, hugging her back.

"Our table is ready. We were just waiting for you to be seated," she says helpfully.

"Right this way," one of the hostesses says. I'm not sure what her name is, but I've seen her around. She's wearing black leather from head to toe, and I can't help but giggle at the look on Mel's face. I can't wait until she sees the rest of the club. Well, not tonight. That'll be up to Coop. But I have a feeling it will be sooner rather than later. They are perfect for each other.

Dinner is the best. Everyone laughs and has a great time. Well, everyone except Ransom. He's always pretty solemn, but when Tessa is around, he's downright grumpy. Those two are like fire and ice. One minute, I think they would be the perfect match. Nights like tonight, I think they would go down in a fiery ball of flames if they ever tried to make something of the chemistry they obviously have. That is one relationship I will never meddle in. I want no part in it.

"Sorry to eat and run, but some of us have to work," Jasper says as he gets up from his chair. He walks around the table and leans over me to give me a side hug. I return the hug and giggle when Colt lets out a little growl. Jasper has become like a big brother to me over the weeks, and I'm lucky to have him in my life. He's an awesome guy and is so caring. He deserves a babygirl who will love him and his overprotective nature.

"Thanks for coming, Jasper."

"Wouldn't have been anywhere else. Happy birthday, kiddo."

I wave bye as he leaves and shortly after the whole party breaks up. Coop and Mel are the next to leave. Well, Mel goes to leave, and Coop insists on walking her out. I'm pretty sure it was more about keeping her from stumbling upon the club proper than her safety, but I'll take it either way. It's one small step towards them, realizing what is right in front of them.

Ransom growls a happy birthday at me, then storms off towards the club. He's not in his work shirt, and I have to wonder if he's going to be playing. If he is... who is it with? Maybe he's just going to sit somewhere and glare at Tessa. He helped keep me safe for weeks without complaint and refused any sort of compensation from me for it. He's a great man... just gruff and grumpy.

"What are your plans for the night?" Tessa asks with a playful smirk.

I shrug. "I'm not sure. Swinging?"

Colt laughs. "Is that what you want to do for your birthday?"

I lick my lips and look up at him. "Maybe?"

"I guess we could change plans."

"I don't think I'm going to be swinging tonight, Tessa," I say, completely distracted by my sexy boyfriend.

Tessa walks away with a laugh.

"Are you ready to play?" Colt asks. "Someone has a birthday spanking coming to her."

"Yes!" My response is so quick and enthusiastic that he laughs.

"Let's see if you're so excited after twenty-eight swats."

My eyes grow wide. "Twenty-eight?"

"One for every year you've been on this Earth, beauty."

He holds me close and kisses me sweetly, then bends at the knee and throws me over his shoulder, carrying me out of the restaurant and to a private room. I giggle when people whistle and hoot at us as we pass.

Colt doesn't put me down until we are locked inside a private room—the Wonderland room, my favorite. He sets me on my feet then shrugs out of his suit jacket. I watch his muscles flex as he slowly rolls up his shirtsleeves. I think this might be the sexiest part of getting ready for a spanking. Especially a funishment like I'm getting tonight.

My core clenches at the look of fire in my boyfriend's

eyes. He's in full-on daddy mode, and it's everything my naughty thoughts could have dreamed up and better. Once his sleeves are expertly rolled, showing off his muscular forearms, he starts stripping me to my panties and bra. Then he has me completely naked and over his lap.

I'm breathless with anticipation as he lovingly strokes my backside. "Look at this pretty pale canvas ready for me to paint."

He gives me a small swat that makes me tense from the surprise of it, but I immediately relax. His hand comes down again and again in light, teasing smacks as he warms me up. I moan when Colt's fingers trail between my cheeks then to my pussy. His fingers slide through my slick folds and circle my clit before dipping inside me. I push back against his hand, wanting more.

Of course, he pulls his hand away and continues my spanking, leaving me wanting, but at the same time craving more of his firm hand. He increases the power behind his strokes until they are hard and painful, but I'm riding that invisible line between pain and pleasure so it's all just pleasure.

"Twenty-seven," he says before spanking directly over my sit spot, then he spanks the other side. "Twenty-eight."

His hand lovingly caresses my heated bottom, and I groan. I relax into his lap, feeling nothing but the high of endorphins. My pussy is so wet, my thighs are slick with my cream. I squeal and arch off his lap when there is a sharp pain on my bottom.

"Can't forget the pinch for good luck," Colt says with a chuckle.

"Mean, daddy." I reach back and rub the spot he pinched.

I don't get away with it for long before he has both my hands pinned to the small of my back in one of his. Then his fingers are at my pussy, stroking and teasing me until I'm wriggling like a wanton mess.

"Please, daddy..."

Colt puts me out of my misery and thrusts two thick fingers into my pussy. My body is so primed that I'm crashing into an orgasm within mere seconds. "Oh, God!" I scream as he keeps fingering me right through my release.

The next thing I know, I'm flat on my back on the bed, and he's between my legs with his mouth on me. He's licking and teasing my pussy until I'm thrown over the edge yet again.

"That's two," he growls against my pussy.

I blink down at him in confusion.

"Birthday orgasms, babygirl," he says with a sexy smirk.

My eyes widen as my sex-hazed brain catches up with what he's saying. "You don't mean..."

"Don't I though?"

"You'll kill me," I groan when his fingers enter me again. He finds my g-spot and thrusts against it on every stroke. "Oh, God..."

My back arches, and my hands fist the blankets below me. "That's three," he says smugly.

I collapse back to the bed, nearly half-dead from pleasure and we've barely started. Thankfully, he kisses his way up my body, giving me a slight reprieve from the sexual onslaught. He kisses each nipple, then moves to my lips. I can taste myself, and, like always, it turns me on. I love the dirtiness of it. Despite being completely sated, I still crave more.

His fingers slip back between my folds and he lightly circles my clit.

"Daddy, it's too much. I can't."

"Just relax, babygirl. I'll take care of you."

He kisses me soft and slow while rubbing those maddening circles around my button. The pleasure grows and grows until it feels bigger than me. Bigger than everything. I release the bedding and thread my fingers through Colt's hair, holding him to me as I kiss him hungrily. The heat rises up inside me until I'm exploding into a million bright shining pieces.

He stands from the bed, licking his fingers clean of my release as he slowly undresses. I watch with hooded eyes as his muscled body comes into view. His cock springs free when he pulls his pants and boxers down, and I moan at just the sight of his thick length.

"Do you like that, naughty girl?" he growls.

"You know I do."

With a sexy smirk he crawls over me, running his tongue up my body from belly button all the way to my lips until he's kissing me again. I wrap my legs around his hips, welcoming him inside me. He slowly presses his cock inside one inch at a time, stretching me with his thickness.

"Fuck, you're so tight. Always so tight for me."

"Only you, daddy."

With a low growl, he thrusts harder. "No one else will ever know the sweetness of this pussy."

I wrap my legs around him tighter, moving with his

punishing thrusts. I scratch my nails down his back, losing myself to the moment. He grabs my wrists, pinning them to the bed, then he leans in close and kisses me. I breathe him in, returning his kiss as he slows his thrusts into something slower, sweeter. He buries himself deep then grinds against my aching clit. Within moments I'm on the edge of the abyss again.

"Daddy!"

Colt nips at my bottom lip. "That's it, babygirl, come on my cock. Come for me."

"Yesss..." I hiss.

He crushes his lips back to mine as our hips move in tandem. It's a dance we've perfected. One that drives us both to the very edge of sanity. Our kiss turns almost feral with its intensity. It's teeth and tongue and passion.

He slips a hand between us, using two fingers to press against my clit and rub tight circles. I explode. It's the supernova of orgasms. I come harder than I've ever come in my life. My vision goes black, and the air seizes in my lungs. It's so intense, my mouth opens in a silent scream. There's no air to make any noise left in my lungs.

"Fuck, baby," Colt grunts as his cock jerks inside me, filling me with his release.

He collapses to the bed beside me and pulls me into his arms. I roll against him, panting for breath.

"Wow."

Colt chuckles. "Five..."

My body is still wracked with shivers and aftershocks from the most powerful orgasm of my life, and he's just told me in four little letters that he's not nearly done with me. "I don't think..."

"We have all night, babygirl."

"How about all weekend?"

He laughs outright. "Okay, all weekend. Such a hardship it will be to spend the weekend between your sexy thighs."

I giggle, feeling breathless and giddy with my love for this man.

"Thank you for the best birthday ever, daddy."

"You're welcome, beauty. I love you."

"I love you too, Colt. Always."

The End

Want more from Colt and Darlene? Check out their bonus story or find it here: https://BookHip.com/XHQFV

Want another daddy dom? Check out Daddy's Obsession.

ALSO BY RORY REYNOLDS

CONTEMPORARY ROMANCE

Babygirl for Christmas

Daddy's Temptation

Daddy's Obsession

Daddy's Treat

Daddy's Princess

Losing Her Heart

Making Her Mine

Earning Her Love

Chasing His Forever

His Firecracker

His Hellcat

Claiming His Wife

Just Married

Dirty Girl

DARK CONTEMPORARY ROMANCE

Unforgettable

PARANORMAL ROMANCE

Dragon's Thief

Dragon's Curse

Dragon's Hope

Dragon's Ruin

Dragon's Treasure

Dragon's Fire

ABOUT THE AUTHOR

Rory Reynolds is a stay-at-home mom of two little monsters. She's a ravenous reader of romance and firmly believes that you can never have too many book boyfriends.

She writes feisty heroines, alpha heroes, and panty drenching smut with happily ever afters.

SUBSCRIBE to my newsletter and get a free book.
http://roryreynoldsromance.com

Printed in Great Britain
by Amazon